QUIET,
PLEASE

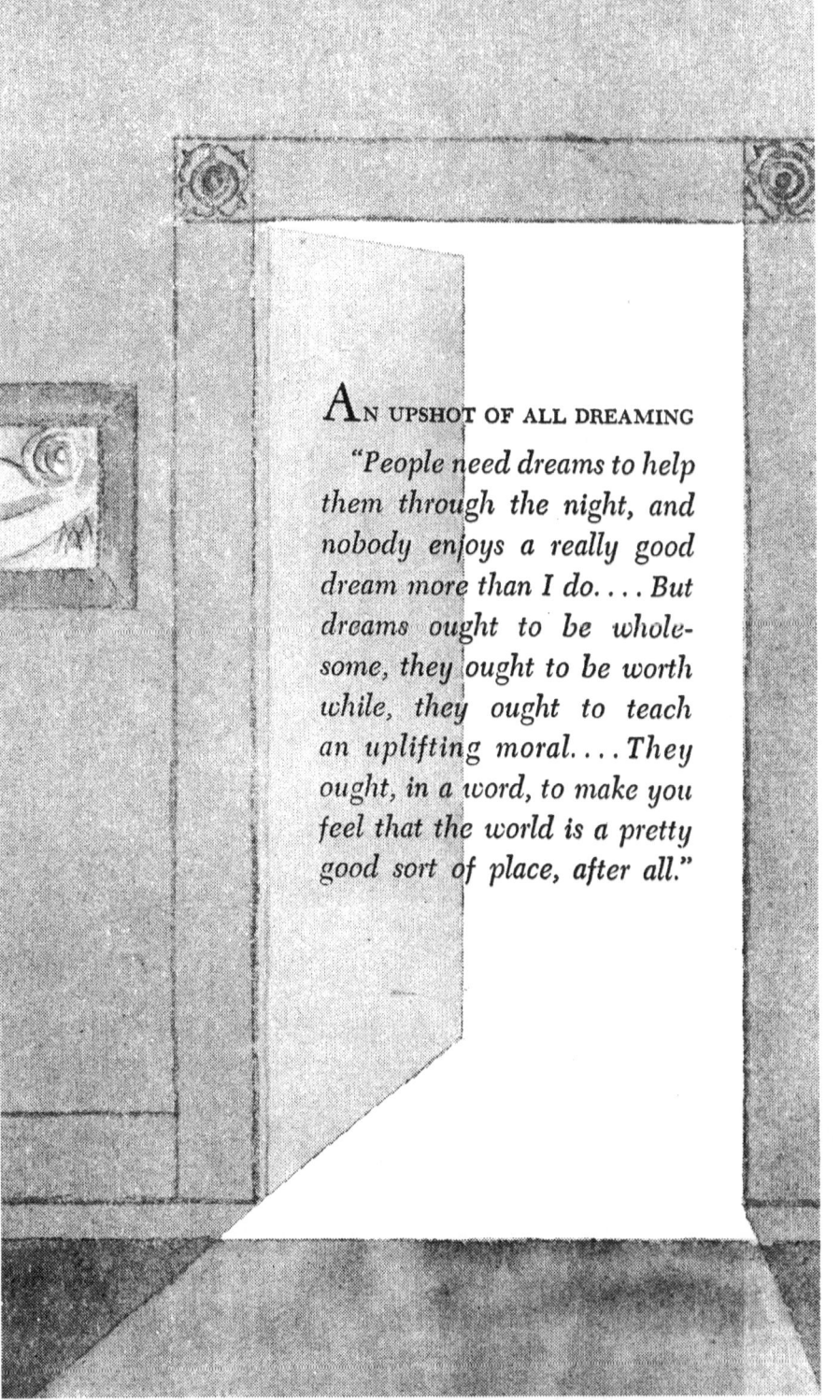

An Upshot of All Dreaming

"People need dreams to help them through the night, and nobody enjoys a really good dream more than I do. . . . But dreams ought to be wholesome, they ought to be worth while, they ought to teach an uplifting moral. . . . They ought, in a word, to make you feel that the world is a pretty good sort of place, after all."

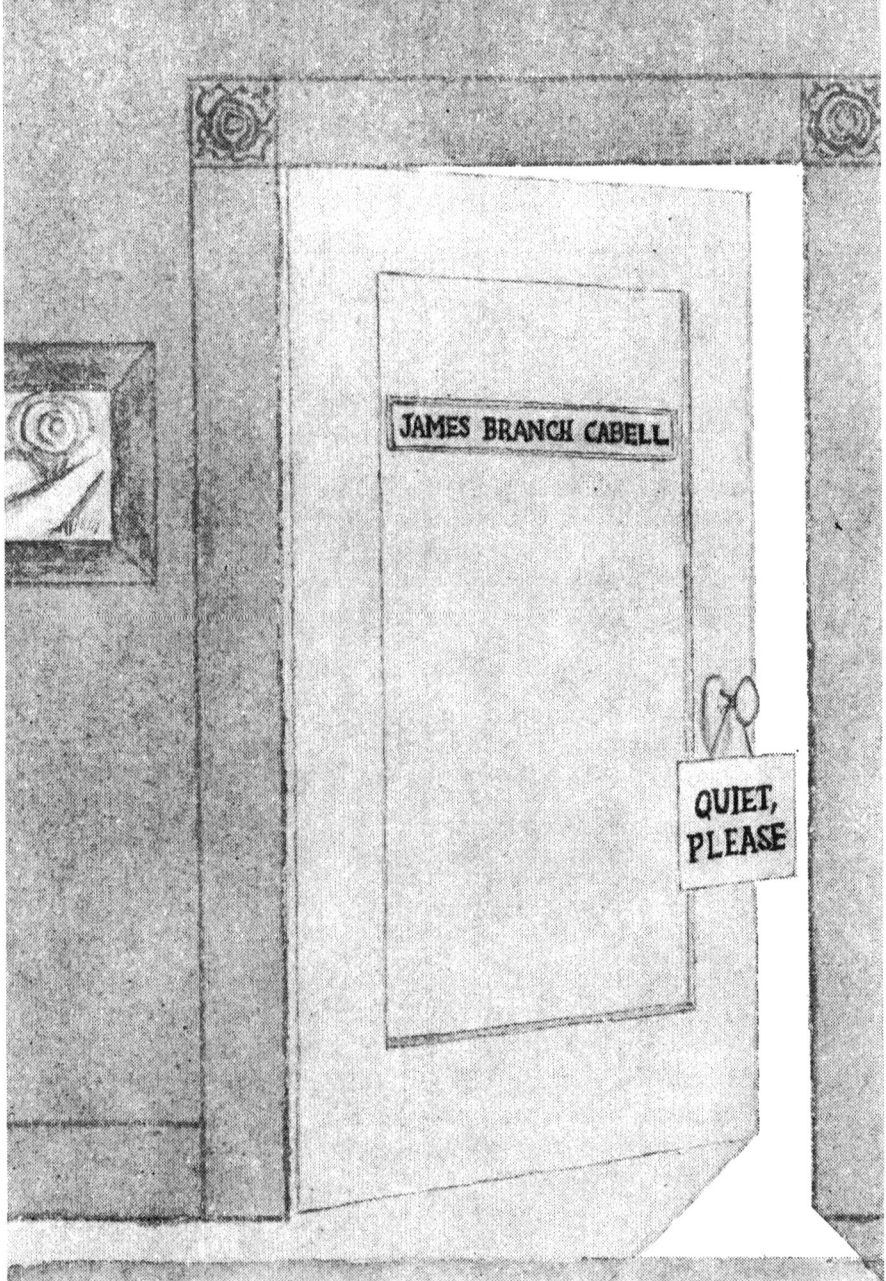

DESIGNED *by H. S. Haines, with* DRAWINGS *by Richard Neidhardt.*

Published by
Wildside Press
P.O. Box 301
Holicong, PA 18928-0301 U.S.A.
www.wildsidepress.com

Books by James Branch Cabell

Biography of the Life of Manuel

BEYOND LIFE ★ FIGURES OF EARTH ★ THE SILVER STALLION ★ THE WITCH-WOMAN ★ DOMNEI ★ CHIVALRY ★ JURGEN ★ THE LINE OF LOVE ★ THE HIGH PLACE ★ GALLANTRY ★ SOMETHING ABOUT EVE ★ THE CERTAIN HOUR ★ THE CORDS OF VANITY ★ FROM THE HIDDEN WAY ★ THE JEWEL MERCHANTS ★ THE RIVET IN GRANDFATHER'S NECK ★ THE EAGLE'S SHADOW ★ THE CREAM OF THE JEST ★ THE LINEAGE OF LICHFIELD ★ STRAWS AND PRAYER BOOKS ★ TOWNSEND OF LICHFIELD, PREFACE TO THE PAST, BETWEEN DAWN AND SUNRISE (*with* JOHN MACY)

The Nightmare Has Triplets

SMIRT ★ SMITH ★ SMIRE

Heirs and Assigns

HAMLET HAD AN UNCLE ★ THE KING WAS IN HIS COUNTING HOUSE ★ THE FIRST GENTLEMAN OF AMERICA

It Happened in Florida

THE ST. JOHNS (*with* A. J. HANNA) ★ THERE WERE TWO PIRATES ★ THE DEVIL'S OWN DEAR SON

Their Lives and Letters

THESE RESTLESS HEADS ★ SPECIAL DELIVERY ★ LADIES AND GENTLEMEN

Virginians Are Various

LET ME LIE ★ ANOTHER BOOK ABOUT HER (*unpublished*) ★ QUIET, PLEASE

Upon Genealogy

BRANCHIANA ★ BRANCH OF ABINGDON ★ THE MAJORS, AND THEIR MARRIAGES

X, Y & Z

THE JUDGING OF JURGEN ★ JOSEPH HERGESHEIMER ★ TABOO ★ THE MUSIC FROM BEHIND THE MOON ★ BALLADES FROM THE HIDDEN WAY ★ THE WHITE ROBE ★ THE WAY OF ECBEN ★ SONNETS FROM ANTAN ★ SOME OF US ★ THE NIGHTMARE HAS TRIPLETS (*pamphlet*) ★ OF ELLEN GLASGOW, AN INSCRIBED PORTRAIT (*with* ELLEN GLASGOW)

THE CONTENTS

The Head, sculptured by Hollis H. Holbrook,
faces
The Portrait, an Introduction, by Marjorie Burke,
which begins on page XI.

QUIET, PLEASE

THE PORTRAIT

by Marjorie Burke

THE HEAD

DURING THE MONTHS THAT ARE WINTER IN THE North, James Branch Cabell, our most urbane and fastidious writer, makes his residence in St. Augustine, Florida, where he continues his nowadays but little noted or acclaimed work, in rooms overlooking rose bushes and budding magnolias. Mr. Cabell was completing his seventeenth season of winter residence in the Oldest City when I last visited him, and upon this visit I was accompanied by an artist, who was prepared to sculpture a portrait bust of the once so widely talked about if not indeed world-famous author, and by Dr. Fülg, the philosopher of art.

It was during the course of this visit that the conversation took place which has been retold so often since, and at so many removes from the actuality, that it has at last become necessary, for the sake of clarity, to record what was really said. Therefore, though no little time has elapsed since our visit, I shall try to relate the conversation just as it occurred, omitting all elements of the marvelous with which it came to be embellished.

The immediate occasion for our visit had been, as I have mentioned, the artist's desire to make a portrait bust of Mr. Cabell, and it was with a shared excitement that we three made our way to his place of residence. The weather, at this season, had failed to settle into the serenity which is Florida's due, and the sun, despite its favorable location in the early sky, was behaving petulantly, showing itself at instants only. For the most part it played a fitful game with clouds that fluttered in the February wind like grey gulls.

Mr. Cabell, quite alone, awaited our arrival, and from his chair before the open window, which framed him against the leaves and shadows of the garden, he rose and welcomed us severally. At this moment a yellow shaft of sunlight shot through the garden foliage into his corner of the room, and we three then felt as we saw him silhouetted thus against the garden backdrop, that we were in the presence of something which had, in actuality, happened long ago, a certain person or place, which this meeting had chanced to recall.

The artist at first seemed to make the natural mistake of taking our host for Jurgen, for Mr. Cabell has the same ironic smile, never quite passing into laughter, which inspirits that hero, and the artist, ambiguously stirred thereby, became too confused to say a word. I, too, was awed into speechlessness, bitterly regretting the desuetude of my Provençal.

Dr. Fülg, however, possessed verbal resources equal to any occasion; and he in consequence forthrightly stated:

"There have been made many cynical insinuations about the quality of your morality, because of the circumstance that you are frequently exampled as the American Faust. So would you kindly explicate whether you really believe all human activity is as hollow as the sound of the spade digging the grave, or as the wind rushing through empty spaces?"

Whereupon Mr. Cabell spoke, looking at him not directly, but with an obliqueness, as if Mr. Cabell were intent upon matters which he was gathering up into the corners of his vision.

"To a time-tutored pessimist the things of this world appear not unendurably disappointing just as they stand," Mr. Cabell said. "Is not that an authentic morality?"

"Yet Jurgen—" Dr. Fülg began once more.

"Jurgen is more than thirty years old, and so should be able to take care of himself," said Mr. Cabell. "At any rate, in common with the reading public at large, I have not thought about Jurgen for a long while. I have found too many other interests, such as, for an example, this typescript here at my elbow."

"Ah, and what is this new book—what is its title?" we queried.

"Inasmuch as I do not yet know, I cannot amply inform you," he said; and we became differently bemused over this fact.

Without being able to surmise Mr. Cabell's thoughts at that moment, I followed his glance, which was directed toward the open window, where three pale plump pigeons, doubtless in search of shelter from the whirling winds, had alighted upon the ledge. And no sooner had they caught sight of us than they fluttered away toward the garden fountain and perched on the fountain's rim. This fountain, protected from the wind which all the while had been making, in the high tree tops, many sinister sounds, shone among the flowers and agreeably mirrored the garden things in its placid eye.

By this time the artist, who had brought a plaster base banked with some twenty-five pounds of green clay, had begun to model his likeness of Mr. Cabell. The artist had also brought along with him instruments for measuring, for he purposed an accurate portrait.

"Mr. Cabell," Dr. Fülg began again, after a brief meditation, "I know that if it were lawful for writers to write their own civil code, they would have long ago secured for themselves legal guarantees of privacy, despite the fact that not a few, through public indifference, have already enjoyed this privilege in all its bitterness."

"And it is a privilege," said Mr. Cabell drily, "with which I too am not unfamiliar, no, not nowadays."

The artist, meanwhile, had been obliged to place himself between our host and the speaker, in order to encircle Mr. Cabell's head briefly with a tape measure, and since the artist and his victim had become engaged in discussing the most favorable sitting position for the model and the facial expression he should best assume, it is possible they did not catch every word of Dr. Fülg's prelude, though he is a forceful speaker. I, at any rate, was able to hear him distinctly.

"To be brief," Dr. Fülg continued, "I would say that a writer's privacy is a self-evident truth which should induct every consideration of a writer. The great Goethe has adaged that whoever wants to understand a poet must travel in the poet's land. But this warning is as misleading as true, since the possibility of any other person's traveling, except as an excursion tourist, in any poet's land, is always doubtful. This conclusion I have drawn from a careful study of your work."

Then Dr. Fülg, opening the Cabell book he had brought with him, became so engrossed in trying to find apt references for his opinions that he forgot his audience, who were each intent on the progress of the sculpture. It was not until our attention was once more drawn toward the garden, where a sudden inrush of yellow butterflies had stirred up a widespread fluttering among the leaves, that Dr. Fülg again took up the thread of his discourse.

"And while it is difficult to find one's way around the poet's land," he said summarily, "it is

yet more difficult to find the poet, although he
dwells there, if anywhere. Sometimes the poet's
landscape is merely a fixed idea, in which case
both poet and traveler are each likely to complain,
with justice, that a monotonous world may be dull.
Some poet-worlds turn out to be only waiting-
stations on timeworn roads, where the poet wastes.
Some are fashion resorts, and some are cemeteries.
However, in none of these categories, Mr. Cabell,
am I willing to place your work."

Here Dr. Fülg paused, for he was no less breath-
less than we were, and the artist made use of this
opportunity to take some photographs of Mr.
Cabell for subsequent use in finishing the portrait.

Then Dr. Fülg, with earnest directness, again
addressed the author, saying: "While I am unable
to connect you with any of the better-known
American literary lineages, I have indeed been
able to hit upon, while discoursing with you today,
what I feel to be the surface of a quality, and I
hazard that no person will disagree with me when
I assign your art to the category of irony."

After having placed the book on the table Dr.
Fülg, judiciously accepting our silence as acquiescence, made ready to continue. He rose from his
chair and, either because of his own zeal, or because he was becoming infected with our own
incipient restlessness, began to pace quietly back
and forth among us. The sequel of his lecture was

thus delivered, in its entirety, after the manner of the peripatetics:

"Irony, Mr. Cabell, is the most distinctive of literary qualities and it is at the same time the most elusive of definition, since its essence is its own paradox, whereby it expounds itself in a dualism."

At this point Mr. Cabell, who is a professed admirer of eloquence, observed our philosopher with close attention.

"The strangest property of irony," Dr. Fülg went on to assure us, "is that it evades description by the ordinary propositional discourse. (It reveals its existence, classically, only through dialogue.) Accordingly, Mr. Cabell, the clue to your method is found in your ready and facile conversation."

Edifying and correct as are Dr. Fülg's theories, I must confess that my thoughts, though against my will, had been again errantly wandering into the garden where the bands of butterflies exhibited, with unreserve, their joyous freedom of wings.

The yellow butterfly is not a rarity in Florida. It flies with the warm south wind, to whose gentle current it keeps pace, and it comes to earth only when the wind fails or blows a gale. The protected garden would provide, in times of stress, an ideal refuge for these aerial migrants, and I surmised

that they might well have used the garden for this
purpose on earlier occasions. Mr. Cabell, at any
rate, appeared to accept their visitation as a matter
of course, and even if I had been tempted to question him regarding the cause of the bright flurry
which now suffused the exterior air, Dr. Fülg's
voice, which is, as I have before mentioned, com-
pelling, must have soon recalled me to more
serious matters.

"The method of irony," he was saying, "is,
moreover, both cleansing and clarifying. Irony is
the greatest teacher, though it is not didactic. It is
the greatest pedagogue, though not pedantic. Do
but consider how Fate, who governs all of us, is
the supreme ironist. 'Man errs, so long as he
strives,' as Goethe says, and who other than Fate,
who brings all to naught, leveling the great of the
world with the small, can sufficiently impress upon
us the vanity of our striving, the vastness of our
error?"

I believe we were all sufficiently disinclined
to contravert so much critical weight, but before
we could give vent to any of our conclusive feel-
ings, the argument, with no signs of subsiding,
had once more resumed its torrential course.

It was perhaps only through an equally relent-
less ardor that the artist managed to attend to the
human semblance that was taking shape under his
hands. But the air was sultry and he complained

that the clay had become perverse and the lighting
unstable. He peered closely at his model, then at
the clay, then out the window, but an uneasy
wrinkle remained in his brow.

The butterflies, which had but lately filled the
garden, had fled the air and had hidden in the
shadows somewhere, and the busy clouds had
spread themselves like a thin veil over the sky. The
wind had ceased. A filtered yellow light glowed
in the garden and shone into the room, revealing
the things inside and the things outside with an
equal and strong intensity. A body of damp but
warm air had crept through the open window.

"And thus Fate, as an ironist, is equalled only
by you, Mr. Cabell," Dr. Fülg was saying. "For
does not she, like you, make puppets of her women
and men? Like you, Fate exerts her talents pref-
erably on the individual whose voice has an all-
confident ring, an Oedipus the King, for example:
a person who is alone in his ignorance of his own
ignorance. And is not the most attractive and
dramatic advantage of the ironic position the fact
that while the onlookers, like the author, are fully
aware of the victim's mistaken opinion of himself,
it is only with difficulty that the victim is able
to learn of his own erroneous and ridiculous
situation?"

Dr. Fülg now looked at each of us in turn for
an answer; and the silence he met was so unani-

mous that with an ill-concealed note of triumph he
forged on to the end.

"Irony, as your art well reveals, Mr. Cabell,
proves that any assertion is dogmatic and one-
sided, and vulnerable to contradiction. Irony con-
jures a bipartient vision of reality, however, and
therefore the ironist, I contend, is the only rational
artist. With his grasp of reality's double value, he
alone is able to whittle a man down to his proper
size and place. Only the ironist can create an art
of harmony and beauty. For a symmetry, after all,
needs two sides. And this, it seems to me, and I
think you may agree, Mr. Cabell, is the correct
interpretation of your method. Of course, much
more needs be said, to complete our discussion of
ironic art, but I do not wish to become tiring."

"After having published some fifty-odd books
and booklets in the course of less numerous years,"
said Mr. Cabell, "I am not unprepared to admit
that, just at times, even the revered art of criticism
may become tiring."

The artist, seated opposite our host, sat back to
survey the progress of his work. "I believe this is
turning out to be a fairly literal portrait," he said,
yet sounding as if he were not quite so sure; and
he added anxiously: "An advantage in working
with clay is that it takes any impression easily."

Mr. Cabell regarded the clay with a not un-
mixed admiration. "Yes," he said, "it does resemble

that green mud in which the creative effort is said to have committed its first indiscretion, euphemized as Adam. Yet perhaps it is therefore all the more suitable as material for the invidious candors that you are perpetrating."

"But in this light the head does not appear quite the same as it was before," exclaimed the artist, raising a perplexed and jealous eyebrow at his recalcitrant creation. "And I am not sure that even your appearance, Mr. Cabell, has not altered a little, in this light," he added defensively.

Mr. Cabell thereupon viewed the back of the green head with curiosity as the artist moved it closer to the window, and then Mr. Cabell obliged the artist by moving his own chair forward. Sitting face to face with his effigy, Mr. Cabell's expression did, this time, alter, unmistakably. It showed, in fact, a degree of alarm. The back of the head he had viewed tolerantly, though without undue interest, as it took shape, but now, in scrutinizing its features, his own assumed a severity not impressed in the clay.

"What do you think of it?" asked the perplexed artist, stepping aside as if he wished for nothing so much as to disclaim all responsibility for his handiwork.

"I confess to a not whole-hearted approval," said Mr. Cabell, looking at the face uncordially.

Then spoke a voice which, had we not been

partially prepared, by Dr. Fülg's instruction, to give ear to the most improbable and far-fetched nonsense, might have caused us some discomfort.

"Since you are so broadminded where others are concerned, O friend," said the voice, "why be such a severe critic of yourself—why condemn, as a fault, my faithfulness to you?"

Of the voice's possessor, had we at first any doubt, we were speedily apprised, when Mr. Cabell, looking at the head, gave it answer clearly.

"I can but ask you to consider the truism," said Mr. Cabell, "that had I been your creator, do you take my word for it, you would have been turned out quite differently."

"I am your own image, with exactitude, though," replied the head, "created to look just as you are."

"Consider yet again," said Mr. Cabell, "how the practice of creating in one's own image, while backed by divine authority, is not always in the best conceivable taste, whether from the viewpoint of modesty or of aesthetics. I suspect it has produced much of what is found objectionable in things as they are—such as a provoking monotony, a tedious sameness, an irritating repetitiousness, and, in brief, the characteristics of mankind at large."

"Yet do you be solaced with the reflection," counseled the head, "that to no other *man* do you bear a resemblance. So I have heard from the best authorities, and my own experience confirms the fact."

"I can see that, in addition to your physical discrepancies," said Mr. Cabell, "you lack veracity in speech also. It was about Socrates that somebody or other wrote 'he resembles no other man.'"

"On the contrary," objected the head, "my historical perspective, at least, has suffered no foreshortening, and I am well-versed in both oral tradition and learned bookish lore. I distinctly recall that you also have been likened to those Silenus statuettes esteemed by the Athenians—statuettes constructed to conceal, in their interiors, every manner of beautiful objects, the delight and wonder of all those persons who took the trouble to find them."

"You are guilty of a grave anachronism," Mr. Cabell replied, "in addition to—such is my very earnest hope the more intently I consider you—a large deal of physical slander."

"Do you be candid, though, and admit, there is a resemblance," enjoined the head aggrievedly.

"Candor was never a social virtue," Mr. Cabell replied; "and my imitators have not ever delighted me."

"Sir," said the head, "I regard your remark as an affront, and here, in self-defense, I must draw a line. Devoted as I am to your special form, we must remain, in one or two other respects, at perpetual odds. I am unable to emulate, for example, your perverse passion for avoiding the commonplace. I am incapable of discrediting, as you evidently do, the ordinary passions which inflame human breasts, such as greed, hate, and ambition. I have not the capacity, as you have, to render myself superior to the humble joys afforded by the humdrum world into which men and women are ejaculated. But your knowledge and art are each of the head, I suspect, and not of the heart, and to be candid I find it difficult to believe seriously in the flesh-and-blood of your creativeness."

So much spoke the head, with some heat.

"That is a reproach, my green humiliater, which very many other critics no less verdant have voiced not infrequently," Mr. Cabell said.

"Does there not remain, however," said the head, "a still more serious charge against you, which has never been sufficiently cleared?"

"And what is that?"

"That you did not heed the behests of Diotima? —Or was she Ettarre?"

Then with a sigh Mr. Cabell asked: "Is it not becoming an inconvenience, not here to say a nuisance, that we both prefer the raising of a question to the settlement of an issue? I think that at this rate we shall never get anywhere in particular."

"So it would appear," the head said.

"Therefore, in the high cause of common-sense," Mr. Cabell continued, "do you agree to answer a question or two. And after that, you may question me, if you indeed wish to keep on talking and talking forever."

"I consent," said the head; "so do you now ask your first question."

"Why, to begin with," said Mr. Cabell, "do you explain to me just what and just whose injunction I am supposed to have disobeyed."

"Very well," said the head. "Often, in your earlier years, she whom you have called the witch-woman spoke to you in confidence, sometimes appearing along with your dreams, sometimes meeting with your quietest noontime thoughts, and what she said was ever the same."

"And what were her words?"

" 'Do you compose and practice music,' she exhorted; and her words were ever the same."

Mr. Cabell then asked: "And did I not at once, and ever since, and do I not even now, attempt to obey her?"

"You have labored to do her no dishonor," the head replied. "You erected a society of beautiful people who lived beautifully, since this work seemed to you the true import of her command. Through the years you have bestirred yourself in single service to the witch-woman, for you believed that the true practice of music consisted in this homage."

"And was I not correct?" Mr. Cabell asked.

"It seemed that you were," the head answered. "For you have builded up many melodies upon pillars of parable. And thus you have charmed your listeners, even as did Silenus, though you played on words instead of on pipes. Your arguments in favor of the rational life and of conformity have been persuasive, for they have been grounded in the firmest artistic illusions. Still, I do wonder, O my friend, whether you have yet played truly, or whether she meant, really, that other music, which we have left unmentioned."

"And what music is that?" Mr. Cabell asked.

"I mean," the head replied, "that dangerous far-off music which sounds between the stars and in the tops of trees; the lonesome, prophetic, possessive music which has no words, and which abhors conformity."

"I have heard of such music," said Mr. Cabell, with a trace of reserve in his manner. "But what has it to do with my writings?"

"Nothing," the head answered. "And that is my point, precisely. For you advocate conformity, you dwell always upon the material smug comfort and the alleged wisdom of doing that which seems expected."

"Now, at long last, you are beginning to make a rational use of your powers of speech," Mr. Cabell said, "by deviating into the comprehensible. And you charge me with that to which I with frankness plead guilty."

Then Mr. Cabell, concerned for his other guests, ordered refreshments served, and said he regretted the interruption in our visit. Whereupon we each assured Mr. Cabell that we had never before met with such delightful entertainment; that we had expected nothing of the sort; and we begged him, with every urgency, not to put an end to the conversation.

Mr. Cabell yielded to our importunities, and agreed to continue the talk, but only upon the condition that we, too, were willing to participate. He afterwards solicited the artist to resume his work whensoever the artistic impulse should so move him, and Mr. Cabell added that he felt certain that a small amount of romanticizing, particularly as to the amount of his hair, would cause the head no discomfort; hinting, with a profound delicacy, that personal vanity, even when it had become merely an academic weakness, need not always be sacrificed to an abject realism.

After tea had been served, and after we had helped ourselves generously of the cakes, Mr. Cabell said:

"I think we may now resume our discussion, and indeed, with favorable luck, we may even find out just what it is all about."

Whereupon we each looked at one another severally, and then intently toward the opaque sky, and remarked that the room was a shade darker. We cited our varying reasons why we thought it was going to rain instantly or clear up, and in this way we speedily arrived at the conclusion, beyond which there was no other, that among all strange and improbable phenomena Florida weather ranks foremost.

The head heard us out without demur, before it spoke what was in itself.

"Now, my friend," it said to Mr. Cabell, "do you bear in mind our agreement that when you had finished with questioning me, and I had finished answering, I could put questions to you; for I greatly desire to question you regarding the music which you would not discuss."

"What did you wish to know about it?" Mr. Cabell asked.

"I wish to know if it is that which you neglected to compose and to practice," the head replied.

"Very well," Mr. Cabell assented. "Yet this music is, did you not say, a most wild and dangerous music?"

"It is, as I have told you," the head replied, "a weird and lonely music which you are accused of neglecting, but a high and mighty music, the first and the most powerful, beyond which there is nothing more to compose or to practice. And I doubt that you can clear yourself, inasmuch as he who is possessed by this music is known to lose all concern for the morrow, to forsake his fireside, and to forget his civic duty. I grant that you have never meddled overmuch with politics, but even so, the fact that he who has become enkindled by the breath of this high music must henceforward rave in prophecies which appear to be nonsense, because nobody can understand them, is a matter sufficient to blast your hopes of acquittal."

"I really do delight in your manner of talking," said Mr. Cabell handsomely.

"Because, O friend," the head continued, "I fear you will never consent to foam at the mouth. Incoherence, to put it frankly, is not your forte. It is, moreover, notorious that you have poured no libations to Discord. You have been likewise ungracious to Folly. And though I am confident that no one else has more attentively commemorated the victories gained daily by these great deities, and though I venture to add, in your defense, that you have deflected from their worship no person who was not already inclined toward such blasphemy, yet do I despair of your case when I think about the worst of your faults."

"And which of that rude multitude do you consider to be the chief?" Mr. Cabell asked.

"That than which there is nothing more damaging, O my friend. It is that inasmuch as you remain obstinately unlearned in the art of writing words without meaning, I gravely fear lest your wits will, in the end, avail you but little to compose that wild and wordless distant music with whose neglect you are now charged."

"But no one of us is sure what you mean"— here Dr. Fülg broke in. "Is not this music a sound, or sounds?"

"Indeed it is," the head replied—"sounds of a far-off region where few have been."

"Then inasmuch as the place is ill-known," Dr. Fülg continued, "is it marvelous that those who are afar from and below the place, yet who sometimes hear its music, should feel unsettled, recognizing in it nothing familiar?"

"That is true," interrupted the head, rather over-zealously. "For example, it chanced that I once heard a griffin's bark, and that was before I knew it was a griffin barking. The sound fretted me deeply until I found out to whom the bark belonged."

—"And being possessed by this first and most powerful music, which they do not understand," said Dr. Fülg, disregarding the head and addressing Mr. Cabell, "is it any wonder that they should forsake their firesides and forget their civic duties, and uttering sounds without meaning, wander about the face of earth seeking the place to which the music belongs?"

But the head was beforehand with an answer. "I concede they must do so out of necessity," it said. "And yet . . . yet, while it is beyond question that my twin here is thoroughly acquainted with that remote and lofty region, and while it is quite obvious that he has done very little in his life besides re-echoing its primal and most powerful music, yet does he disclaim its practice; he evades answering me as to the music which abhors compromise; and I most heartily wish I might have made use, at some point in the conversation, though I now forget at just what point, of my right to question him as to yet another allied matter."

Then the head became silent and looked as if it were pondering to the end a long and devious thought somewhat sullenly.

"Why, but truly now, if I do not allow to this loquacious and pig-headed green monster his alleged right to be prying into wholly personal matters," Mr. Cabell explained to us, as if in confidence, "then I fear he may fly into a huff, or into a tantrum, or perhaps even into a dudgeon. And it is my feeling that any one of these three aviational outcomes might very well lead him to misrepresent me yet more flagrantly than—to my stubborn conviction—he does already."

"Since then you permit me just one personal question, pardonable on the grounds of my unique relationship to you," the head replied, "I entreat you to tell me why, in the vast bulk of your publishings, you have not ever included a book about that of which you must have the most nearly complete knowledge—namely, about yourself."

"Why, but for one matter," said Mr. Cabell, "I prefer to avoid telling falsehoods. And I do not know of anyone who can afford to be more than partially truthful about himself in public. Yes, and through chivalry alone, do you let me add, have I confined myself to a pronoun wholly masculine."

"Yet do you mistake my meaning," said the head. "In discussing physical events one may well remember that prudence is a virtue; nor is that which happens to a person, or which is done by a person, to be viewed in logic as a part of that person. Rather would I suggest that if only you halt your thoughts as they pass, and speak them just as they occur, you would then contrive, with a peculiar veracity, your own self-portrait and a likeness very far more faithful than your self-conceit can adjudge me to present."

"Yes, and if you would put them into a book," interposed Dr. Fülg, with enthusiasm, "why, but then you would provide a most valuable document for the interpretation of your remarkable literary work."

"In the light of these solicitations, which I incline to receive with not less than ten grains of salt and an equal number of blushes," said Mr. Cabell, "I admit that I have here at my elbow the almost completed typescript of a sort of a something which is not unlike the book you describe. It in fact lacks only some rewriting, along with a brief acrostic to serve as its dedication; and upon this morsel of verse I am now engaged."

"I infer, with a whole-hearted satisfaction," said the head, "that you are doing in this book even as I have exhorted and advised."

"And that you are composing, let us hope, an *Apologia pro Mente Sua,*" said Dr. Fülg, "pursuing your material at random, as your thoughts come to you, and confessing their natural and exuberant course?"

"So it appears," said Mr. Cabell, clearing his throat, "for if the fact at all matters (which I esteem to be dubious), the apparently haphazard style of this book—or to be somewhat more precise, of this booklet—was not unpremeditated."

"Why, then—" said Dr. Fülg.

"It is," said Mr. Cabell, with peevish asperity over having been untimely interrupted, "a bit of writing which aims to record—to record, I repeat, rather than to mimic—the involved and the intricate and the disordered evolution of all reverie, with the casualness, the meanderings of thought, the rude candors, the disconnections, the incessant egotisms, the belated qualifyings, and the revertings (or, here to become technical, the 'cutbacks'), each and every one of them presented more or less as, to my personal finding, they do occur. —Which occurring is not the very least bit (still, just to my personal finding) in accord with that vexed and overvexing abomination known as the 'stream of consciousness' method, do you let me assure you."

"Still—" remarked Dr. Fülg, who did not at all appear to grasp the futility of interrupting an author when once he has begun to talk about himself and his own writings.

"Yet furthermore," said Mr. Cabell, "this book is a but slightly foiled attempt to write 'in character.' I have, that is, I have endeavored vaingloriously to depict myself as being all that which I ought to be—in my present-day lack of acclaim, I mean—as being a disgruntled and embittered person, a cantankerous babbler, an enraged, forever sneering, obscene egotist, and a self-conscious failure well sunk in age and ability. And here, in the main, I make bold to think I have succeeded."

The head nodded its silent approval. But we,

somewhat more politely, felt called upon to protest against the speaker's injustice to himself.

Whereupon Mr. Cabell sighed; and caressing his typescript, he continued:

"The great trouble, though, in my self-devotion to misanthropy and to embitterment and to pessimism has been that—as I forget who lamented—'a little cheerfulness keeps creeping in,' along with a twist toward the frivolous, because of my all-grateful and my too whole-hearted contentment with human life, as life, by and large, has treated me. I, in brief, have enjoyed living. And I still enjoy it, without violence, admiringly. That I cannot very well help."

The room had become darker as he spoke, although this phenomenon was caused by the thickening shadows of the trees rather than by Mr. Cabell's resignation to a lack of acute unhappiness; and we agreed it was high time to make our departure. Whereupon the artist packed away the head, no longer vocal, which its original, I fear, in wholly outtalking it, had silenced forever, and the three of us left.

So ended the conversation of that day. I have related it as accurately as my memory permits, and I believe that I have omitted nothing of weight or of unimportance.

F_{OR}

the sole possible though somewhat improbable
person

    Most vividly do I, in chief, recall
A tilted chin throughout the far years when,
Regardful of each other, we gave all,
Gave all our lives, to other women and men.

    And vividly I find all rather odd,
Remembering how little then I thought
Ever to love you, or to gain from God
That grace which came to us, unknown, unsought.

Youth is amenable to persuasion in a disastrously large number of matters. Yet upon one single issue youth stays as iron and granite: youth does not ever believe that life serves well enough just as it stands. To conjecture that such is just possibly the case remains the attested hall-mark of middle life. ... Thereafter optimism develops insidiously; and the more lucky among us sink, cackling thinly, into an amiable senescence."

§1. ONE HAS SCRIPTURAL ASSURANCE THAT FOR whosoever survives three score and ten years all the remainder of his living is but labor and sorrow. Yet is it wisdom's part to recall that David, the son of Jesse, was not remarkable for complete truthfulness, either during the conduct of his homicides or throughout his hymn-making. And he spoke here, midcourse in his ninetieth psalm, I submit, with an extreme poetic license.

—Because being rather older than is ordinary isn't, to my finding, no, not of necessity, quite so bad as all that comes to.

To the contrary, there, almost always, I believe, is a certain smugness and a mild sense of individual achievement begotten by the knowledge of having outlived  SOME OF WHICH BORDERS ON EGOTISM

one's seventieth year. I have observed its parade by any number of septuagenarians. Yet, as concerns myself (whom I confess herewith to be my leading theme hereinafter), I at least was not over-conscious of this small vanity upon the most unhappy birthday of my life, when I came to my Davidicly permissible three score and ten an exact two weeks after those so wholly dear imperfections which for so long a while, and which

alone, had made living worthy of endurance—
because it was thus that the grim outcome then
seemed to me, howsoever transiently—had been
buried in Emmanuel churchyard. I preferred not
to go on living after the death of my wife, or
rather, to be wholly accurate about it, of my first
wife.

Howsoever transiently, do you let me repeat.
—Because by-and-by, very gradually, during the
gray months which followed, why, but then as I
awakened from the deeper stupors of misery and
of solitude, I appeared, somehow, to have entered
into a new atmosphere of acquiescence with
what, at this season, I took to be life's over plainly
revealed, naked and brutal rŭthlessness. Life had
hurt me, I felt, to the utmost extent of life's
malignity. And so, all further misfortunes must,
by comparison, become trivial. Whatever might
happen to me henceforward could not, not really,
matter.
—Which was far from logic, of course; it was
an emotional response to my entire anguish. And
yet (as I noted with some interest), yet I found
this cast of mind to be alike a tonic and a narcotic
throughout that upset and bereft and bewildered
period during which I attempted to confront unaided, but how very futilely, an existence which
the not ever tiring, all-loving woman—whose be-

loved body, once as familiar to me as my own body, now lay remote and motionless and corrupting in Emmanuel churchyard—could not any longer keep cheery and easeful, or superintend.

Today—now that I have regained love, along with a mild share of interest in my fellow creatures, and have yet another highly competent and most dear person born under practical-minded Virgo in complete charge of me and of all my doings—well, but today (with a continuing sense of impersonal detachment from my own merely personal emotions, such as every author acquires by-and-by), today I observe that this half-stunned acquiescence with life, as human life actually if a bit regrettably is, has become alike more genial and a vast deal more comprehensive.

—For I lack, so do I reflect, no physical comfort. Unopulently I possess—so far as runs my knowledge—virtually all that for which, after all, at my belated stage of existence, any rational derelict could well ask; and with life, in consequence, I today am satisfied, both tolerably and tolerantly, without any large fervor perhaps but without any tinge of resentment. I have nothing to complain of, I concede, handsomely, the conditions of human life being what they are for each and for all of us when once we have risked being born.

And yet I feel, I feel in some measure, that I am thus nobly broadminded because whatever may happen, or what currently is happening, whether to oneself or to others, or whatsoever is reported to have happened before the mendacities of today's morning paper, they also, had become a part of human history, does not seem so very much to matter, not with its former acute profoundness, after one has passed seventy, and when one of necessity has put aside man's customary delusions concerning tomorrow's being a new and more glorious day.

—Because with one's own tomorrow, and with its imminence, one is but too familiar. And over the future of all other persons likewise, so one now knows, one has not any control. Meanwhile (and yet for no long while) a gentleman will attempt to meet the future with civility.

Thus at any rate does the affair appear to me now that Time has remarked premonitorily but, even so, with a sufficing gentleness,—

"Quiet, please."

§2. ONE, in brief, at what the kindhearted might describe as a comparatively mature age, is able to face the universe, and our human living therein, and even the nature of one's own being, with a contented sense of irresponsibility for these droll phenomena. One adjudges them each and all to be riddles which may, or which may not, have answers; and these answers may, or they may not, be revealed by-and-by. Nothing can be done about it, either way. And in any case, now that memory—after never so many years of unflagging practice in *suppressio veri*—now that memory, I repeat, so tactfully edits the past, one recalls having got a huge deal of pleasure from these same droll phenomena. And in consequence one regards them with a temperate approbation.

I have written, I find—I who with hale good faith have written so very much as to which later on I dissented with a tacit violence—that in old age "optimism develops insidiously; and the more lucky among us sink, cackling thinly, into an amiable senescence." Today I know that optimism is hardly the precise word; for, after seventy, nobody can well hope that any events of an unfettered agreeableness infest the future; one instead inspects tomorrow with a tepid resignation, gloating mildly meanwhile over that which has been wrested from more than twenty-five thousand yesterdays.

—Or at any rate, I do.

§3. I BECOME, it may be your criticism, not thoroughly unegoistic. Yet in this same paragraph must I exhort the rational to squander no large faith upon any writer when once he deviates from egotism. About himself he, just possibly, may, should he so elect and strive earnestly, be telling you the truth. That the odds are strongly against this off-chance, one need hardly point out, in the light of every human being's desire for self-justification, or for self-glorifying rather, which tends always to embellish an attempt at self-portraiture. Still, the chance does exist.

But when a writer touches upon themes other than himself and his own endurances, his own joys, but above all, his own personal delusions, then that chance expires. He henceforward must write as to affairs about which perforce he stays dubiously informed.

—For he, like everyone of us, he too, is serving his life sentence inside the cell which we term a skull. He knows only that which happens inside it. His confinement there may be enlivened, it is questionless, by as many as five radios—which it is our custom, severally, to call sight, or hearing, or touch, or odor, or taste—and the one or the other of them almost constantly fetches in reports as to what is going on outside. Yet would it be over-optimism to fancy that these news announcements all reach the attendant prisoner unmarred by atmospheric conditions, or even that they stay uninfluenced by the whims of their unknown sponsor, Who is under no constraint to be reporting the truth.

About other persons than himself, in fine, nobody knows anything whatever with assurance.
Here is a stark truism from which I deduce that
through egotism alone may any writer hope to
attain veracity or ever to be esteemed credible.
And for this reason, among yet other reasons, do
I (at least hereabouts, at this present writing)
consider egotism to be alike an aesthetic virtue
and, in mere logic, a moral obligation which is
laid upon all persons who desire to avoid re-
peating tarradiddles.

This does not mean, of course, that anybody
should dare unwisely to belittle or to deplore
tarradiddles in their own proper and all-predom-
inant place. There is no waking moment during
which our five frail, limited and inaccurate senses
do not report to us tarradiddles under the august
sponsorship, and with, so one presumes, the approbation of whatsoever force it was that—or
perhaps Who—created us as we are.

Furthermore, there is not any prisoner incar-
cerated in the cell which we term a skull who
does not solace his captivity by investing some
quota of belief in tarradiddles about his captivity
—those highflown fictions as to human living
which make human living endurable, and indeed,
to the best of my experience, a most interesting
and fervent, if inconsequent, performance. About

these "dynamic illusions," however (as my former acquaintance, John Charteris, once described them), I need not speak in this place, after having devoted to them elsewhere the text of an entire book. I prefer, instead, to refer you to the pages of *Beyond Life*, for his comments upon love, chivalry, patriotism, gallantry, virtue, creative literature, religion and yet other amenities of our existence.

§4. HEREABOUTS, though, I am checked by the reflection that remarkably few persons appear to read *Beyond Life*, or any other of my books, nowadays. I cannot wonder reasonably over this omission, in view of the fact that I myself do not ever open these books by choice, but only when I have need to look up some passage or another (as I have been doing lately), in connection with the glad taskwork of writing still another book. Yet do I find it perceptible—here to riot in understatement—that I, who was once a leading personage in and about those scanty playgrounds of human interest which we nickname literature, seem now to have become, for all practical results, unheard-of thereabouts.

To the youthful, or for that matter to the middle-aged, flamboyant virtuosi of literature who at this present instant are discussing the transcendent merits of Francis X. Flubberdub

and Gideon Gibberish and Natalie Babu English,
as well as of Laura Caconym Nugatory (and who
will be joined to other idols long before this is
published), my name, and beyond doubt my
writings, I infer to be unknown, yes, even by
spruce judges who stay always so far too scrupu-
lous-minded to deny being omniscient. Other-
where, a bare handful of senile dodderers do
seem to recall, just here and there, infrequently
and with languor, that once upon a time, a most
ancient time, somebody of my name wrote a very
much overrated something or other which was
called *Jurgen*. Such must, I take it, be regarded
as the extent of my repute, alike among the sten-
torian intelligentsia and as concerns "the reading
public" at large, nowadays.

And to the bleakly rational this must appear a
sad comedown for any writer who in a majority
of our newspapers' book pages and literary sup-
plements, in that ancient time, was spoken of with
fervor, upon every Sunday morning, almost as
often as Jehovah. He was honored by our then
current virtuosi as a supremely gifted prose artist;
as an unequalled satirist; and as an American
Anatole France, as well as an American Walter
Pater, an American Lucian, an American Arthur
Machen, an American Congreve, an American
Oscar Wilde, and an American Swift, so nearly
as I can now recollect his varied prototypes. He

was acclaimed, here to repeat my pet eulogy, as
an ideational oriflamme in the battle of the nine-
teen-twenties against puritanism; and he was
likened to I forget precisely what other large
inaccuracies.

I forget because I do not haunt the cemetery
of my scrapbooks, revisiting it only when a need
arises to verify some date or some far-off happening. But with a suitable gravity, I can recall,
even nowadays, that all these tributes and judicious analogues and ecstatic paeans are to be
found in this cemetery entombed forever.

With the pride natural to a Virginian, I recall
also that by this impostor my native state was
never hoodwinked. His books were not purchased
in Virginia; they were not talked about except,
just in passing, shruggingly; nor at all often were
they even borrowed gratis from his birthplace,
which, through time's purification, had been con-
verted alike into a free public library and a shrine
to the cultural achievements of Major James H.
Dooley in the stock market and in the enlarge-
ment of railways.

Not ever was this ephemera spoken of in the
same breath as were the ingenious Mr. So-and-So
and the scholarly Dr. Somebody-or-Other, or as
were the all-gifted Mrs. What's-Her-Name and
the perhaps yet more widely famous Miss Thin-

gumbob, whensoever their ever-living genius was acclaimed by the exiguous yet exigent "reading public" of Virginia. —Because all these were Virginian writers in whom Virginia might take pride. They wrote real fine books, so you had seen in the *Times-Dispatch,* only last Sunday; and Miller *&* Rhoads (which at this period was Richmond's largest department store) was still selling a whole lot of their books, after having given them an autographing tea-party, with just heaps and heaps of people at it. Thus quoth all Richmond admiringly.

But that pretentious lewd humbug, that midnight assassin, that no doubt homosexual halfwit, who did not even have sense enough to know that —alike in novels and in children's stories and in biographies and in editorials—a Virginian must write always about the beauty and the chivalry and the peerless moral standards and all the yet other outstanding features of Virginia in fiction, why, but he most properly was ignored throughout our fair commonwealth, even from Lee County to Accomack County, except only when in Richmond the élite forgathered to discuss, in happy whispers, the turpitudes of his how very far from private life. —Because he was just like all the Cabell men, only much more so, and in more directions.

Outside Virginia, however—so may I dare

assure a generation who never heard of me—my books were quite highly thought of, here and there, throughout a full decade. In fact, my books became the theme of that which exaggeration might term a nation-wide controversy during this period. And today, to so much of ecstasy and of clangor and of denouncings and of high disputation, Time has whispered,—

"Quiet, please."

§5. WELL, but today, in my unknownness, I find I do not especially regret, or rather, I do not desiderate, as we niminy-piminy "stylists" might phrase it, that put-by pre-eminence into which I was catapulted by accident. Its one pleasing personal feature, to my remembrance, was the attendant plumpness of my royalty statements; and even that led me into incessant trouble with various Internal Revenue Agents, who do not esteem me an alluring quarry today. Otherwise, I found that being a famous writer interfered too much, and far too often, with the pursuit of writing, with my main interest in life.

—Because always and continuously my professed idolaters were attempting to trap me into doing something dislikable and laborious, such as autographing a few dozen first editions (each with an apt individual inscription) or answering the same inane questions over and yet over again,

such questions as I have indicated in *Special Delivery* (if ever, through any out of the way chance,
you have heard of *Special Delivery*), when upon
Saturday after Saturday I replied to my postulants' so repetitious letters; or else into partici-
pating in varied forms of futile time-wasting, such
as fornication with some hitherto unknown
gentlewoman whose husband did not understand
her, or revising a nitwit's typescript, or sharing
"strange pleasures" with Wilde-minded young
men, or addressing book fairs and women's clubs.
Upon one occasion, as I must still recall with an
incredulous shudder, I was invited to speak before a Chamber of Commerce.

I, who was born taciturn, was beset throughout
my heyday by interlocutors desirous, babblingly,
to find out whether I wrote in the morning or in
the evening; what I thought about death and my
ideal woman and capitalism and Calvin Coolidge;
whether my (non-existent) secretary opened all
my letters; what would be the title of my next
book; and who, in my opinion, was the most
promising of our younger Southern writers. Moreover, I, who have always viewed my own personal
appearance with a rational disfavor, was exposed
over frequently to the cruel candors of photog-
raphers and of portrait painters.

And finally, I, who ever since I quitted my last
diapers had been reared alike to be thrifty and

considerate of all persons, including myself, I was faced hourly by the choice between submitting to these tedious evils, along with yet many other requirements no less distasteful, or else of disregarding my own personal bank account (along with my publishers' very faint faith in my common-sense) and the certainty of being adjudged, as my nearer friends among the intelligentsia of Virginia put it, just simply too stuck-up and too swell-headed for anybody to have any least patience with.

—For throughout America these varied fawnings upon "publicity" were, even in my remote heyday, as they continue to be, a recognized branch of authorship. From every well-known writer such antics are not requested; they instead are demanded as a matter of course.

§6. AN AUTHOR NEEDS TO BE PUBLICIZED THUS strenuously and so ignobly, it is my belief, because, to an ever increasing majority of mankind, books tend to seem obsolescent. The most of us today regard books with a dubiousness, with a vital unconcern. They after all have no weighty part in our living.

It may be that reading becomes less and less widely favored as a rational pastime because, instead of browsing over a book, and without any ponderable mental exertion, one nowadays can always be looking at pictures—alike in our moving picture palaces, and in those philanthropic magazines which consist almost wholly of pictures, and in television, and in the pages of comic strips which  disfigure our newspapers, and upon billboards, and in advertising matter of every nature, as well as in the depressing gritty atmosphere of historical museums and of art galleries. Everywhere in our present makeshift for civilization does one face this universal attempt, through the substitution of a picture, or by preference of several pictures, to minimize one's need to read—along with the attendant suggestion that reading is a form

ABOUT
THE CRAFT
OF
SPOILING PAPER

of labor from which one is being spared kind-
heartedly so far as proves possible.

We cannot expect the impressionable and
plastic young, who daily are being reared among
surroundings thus painstakingly pictorial, to
escape being influenced by this ever-present suggestion; nor do they escape. They, to my experience—an experience, do you let me explain,
which includes seven step-grandchildren and several hundreds of their associates viewed at close
quarters throughout the last twenty-five years—
they tend more and more to think about the reading of any printed matter as a bit of taskwork
which now and then one needs to perform for
utilitarian ends, such as acquiring knowledge of
the current baseball scores or being enabled to
scrape through an examination at school or in
college.

An occasional murder mystery, provided always that it be sufficiently ill written, may serve
to kill time—*faute de mieux,* so to phrase it with
ostentation—but only when the book's youthful,
sprawling unentertained reader can think of
nothing else whatever to do. The notion of reading with an attendant sense of aesthetic pleasure
does not seem to these young people comprehensible; or rather, while they may concede
shruggingly the existence of this ancient quaint

practice here and there among their elders, it appears aberrational.

Descending from this immature point of view to lower levels, I notice that our book clubs do not often pretend falsely that their choice of reading matter for this month could be read with enjoyment. They protest instead that it deals with a vital question of the day; or that it gives you the hushed-up facts as to something or other which happened deplorably the day before yesterday; or else that (here to cite their more usual form of tarradiddling) if you are not able to discuss this book, which everybody everywhere is talking about, then your culture will be adjudged deficient.

I deduce, at the dictates of common-sense, that we are creating a nation in which by-and-by the frivolous notion of reading for mere pleasure will rest at one with the wild buffalo and the three cent piece and the great auk in oblivion. And yet I do not quite believe this. I have seen a vast deal too much of man's common-sense and his human logic, and of the way they work out.

I imagine, I grant you, that the average-novel reader—under which head I would rank those thousands upon millions of literate and fairly high-grade morons who today continue to read our better-advertised modern fiction, confessedly, "so as to kill time"—would disappear overnight, in the abrupt fashion of sora, if ever human ingenuity should contrive any other formula for time's trucidation, except reading, which could be attended to, single-handed and quietly, in your own home, or in bed (I mean, of course, without a companion), or for that matter, virtually anywhere else. But as yet, there is no such other formula. And it follows that millions of us who would prefer an avocation less ruinous are led pitiably to impair our not ever over-vigorous mental powers by reading, and sometimes by reading daily, much of the very best-selling American fiction.

For an example, at St. Augustine, in Florida, that haunt of the age-stricken, I now for winter after winter have viewed with compassion I know not how numerous hordes of elderly gentlewomen while they toiled onward through what they would have called, if only they had not been complete gentlewomen, "some damned book or other."

There was nothing else they could do. Arthritis, or "a heart condition," or some other of the degenerative diseases, had checked all physical activity for these aging ladies, beyond their twice-a-week attendance of the current moving pictures, but two blocks distant, and a similarly brief

trudge churchward, in their very best apparel,
every Sunday morning. In fine, they could not
nowadays, as they put it, "get around much"; and
moreover, they were not wanted anywhere.

—For they had no longer any physical attrac-
tions; their intelligence, and far more the sparkle
of their conversation, had never, it is possible,
been noteworthy; their husbands had died long
ago, without, let us hope, any unchivalrous ex-
pressions of relief; whereas their children and
grandchildren, "back home," considered, howsoever tacitly, that Grandmother had become a
decrepit, babbling, tedious nuisance. And in con-
sidering thus, one regrets to add, these defaulters
in proper grand-filial emotions were wholly
correct.

I concede that now and then the infirm, the
pathetic gentlewoman concerned was a once
potential grandmother who had failed, somehow,
in a woman's vital duty, to marry anybody; but
the principle, as well as the impatience of her
nearer relatives, stayed the same.

So every year, in November, Grandmother
would be shipped southward for a winter in
Florida, there to consort with three yet other
put-by grandmothers, or great-grandmothers,
every evening over a card table; to write interminable letters "back home"; to attend church at

eleven o'clock every Sunday morning; to spend
two afternoons of every week at the Matanzas
Moving Picture Theatre; and for the remainder
of every week, either upon the veranda or in the
patio of her hotel, "so as to kill time," to read, and
to read doggedly, all the very latest best-selling
fiction which was being peddled by her book
club, or which had been sent in to her from one
of the two rental libraries upon Avilés Street.
That was too far to walk.

To any author it could not but seem a depressing spectacle, to observe the unhidden disfavor with which these patrons of literature
continued to read onward every day, each one of
them in a so visible, scowling tantrum with the
especial book which she was reading "so as to kill
time."

She did not want to read this book, or for that
matter, any other book. She was deriving from it
no least pleasure, no interest even. But, like my
aforementioned step-grandchildren and their ju-
venile fellows, the poor creature could not think
of anything else whatever to do.

Well, and throughout these United States, I
submit, there are millions like her, not necessarily
in age, or in sex either, but in that habit, enforced
by luckless circumstances, of needing, "so as to
kill time," to read the more popular examples of
our current fiction, of the fiction written by their

mental peers. And I pity, with an admixture of wonderment, all these unhappy drug-fiends.

Yet they account, I suppose, for the otherwise unaccountable prosperity of our book clubs among rational surroundings; and of book clubs there is no self-respecting author but must approve most cordially, without any least unselfish reservations, now that book clubs and moving picture rights have become the main sources of a publisher's possible income, sources which may enable him to recoup his inescapable loss of money, nowadays, so often as he wantons in the extravagance of having, occasionally, a commendable book printed and bound and dust-wrappered and put on sale for considerably less than the manufacturing of it cost him.

Without book clubs and without Hollywood, so do I at any rate reflect, all publishers would now be in bankruptcy, and each of my later volumes in typescript. For this reason, then, should everyone of us acclaim the book clubs, because they aid in the production of books which they do not commend, and which in fact, so runs the colloquialism, they would not touch with a ten-foot pole.

And as go the books which they do commend, but in particular the books which they present as being "the month's choice of our judges," inasmuch as I do not ever feel any more tempted to

read these books than if they had been aspersed
with a Pulitzer prize, so may these books do me
no harm.

—Which recalls the fact that I do not seem
actually to read the entire long way through any
recent book nowadays. To my obsolete standards, almost all the books now being published
by my juniors, by how very much my juniors,
appear botched through their writers' failure to
master, or even to have had a try at, the art of
writing, so far as ever I could understand the principles of writing during the last fifty-odd years
which I have devoted to its study and its practice.

I do not feel, though, not exactly, that I am
right, and that my juniors are in default; but
rather, that inasmuch as their goals are not mine,
oh, most certainly not mine, so now in consequence I may be judging a well-ordered approach
to these goals to be inurbane and gangling. I am
really quite fair-minded about the entire affair;
and I lay aside with benevolence the youngster's
book, with a benevolence very far more nearly
complete than has been my reading of it.

§7. TO THE BOOKS IN WHICH ONCE UPON A TIME I delighted I return with frank trepidation. They but rarely, as we say, hold up.

Now and then, as with Thackeray and Dickens, it is as though I were revisiting a mansion in which I was once a guest, and in which a dear host of ancient inveterate friends yet greet me. More often, as with Sir Walter Scott, I—stultified, stunned, shocked, flabbergasted—I can but dazedly wonder that anybody, even so gullible a person as memory convicts me of having been upon occasions beyond numbering, could have viewed with seriousness any such balderdash, or could ever have accepted without a frenzy of protest any such stilted and clumsy writing or so many persistently inaccurate substitutes for human speech and human behavior.

OF REVERTING TO OLD FRIENDSHIPS

And it would be facile here to list never so many yet other time-devastated idols, deserted now and left unhonored in the jungles of literature so far as goes my personal homage, those writers in whom I once found enjoyment—along with all perfection, too, sometimes—but whom, nowadays, I regard with more or less of the same half-wistful bemuddlement.

Yet one should not be thankless. There was a time, a not unvividly remembered if callow time, when I adjudged well-nigh every one of the Waverley Novels to be magic-haunted. I have followed with a delighted concern the fortunes of Nigel So-and-So (about whose surname I confess my complete ignorance nowadays) in virtually all quarters of Jacobean London; and of Quentin Durward in and about Plessis les Tours and the city of Liége when sinister King Louis the Eleventh and the Wild Boar of Ardennes were misbehaving in these two vicinities. And, with deep zest, I have banqueted at Kenilworth Castle, through the courtesy of the Earl of Leicester, as well as with Saladin, King of Kings, after that more than chivalrous heathen monarch had turned out not, after all, to be the skilled leech Something-or-Other, whose exact physicianary name I, at the instant, forget. I believe it was El Hakim, but I elect not to brave the present-day tediums of *The Talisman* in order to make sure.

Then at Ashby I have broken a lance or so amongst plaudits, and the castle of Torquilstone I have defended with an heroic stubbornness. But above all, throughout an allegedly bonny Scotland which I have never visited in the flesh (nor which, in this special case, has anybody else either) my excursions, once, were no less frequent than extensive, covering as they did a half-dozen

centuries and every known class of society, from
a peasantry somewhat overgiven to pietism and
dialect to royalty *en famille*. And I believed every
stolid, stodgy, pompous paragraph of it, not
noticing that I hobnobbed with wax works.

What improbabilities, what dullnesses, though,
in my time have I not read with a sincere faith
and admiration! One's mind, being merely human,
recoils from a guess at through exactly how many
trillion miles of type my young and as yet unspec-
tacled eyes once travelled, joyously, athwart the
pages of William Harrison Ainsworth, and of Cap-
tain Frederick Marryat, and of Bulwer Lytton—
and of Maurice Hewlett, even in his latter maun-
derings, yes, even of George Eliot likewise—and
of so very, very many other writers whom today I
find to be as sad twaddle as a Congressional
Record or as the effusions of the late Gertrude
Stein and James Joyce. Yet in all these writers
(excluding with shrill emphasis the last-named
pair) I at one season or another delighted. And
the pleasure which they gave me was wholly real,
no matter how flimsy and unenduring may have
been its foundations.

For that pleasure I stay indebted. It may have
been due to the merits of these aforementioned
writers (whom I have named at random from a
huge host of their fellows in my present-day dis-
esteem), to merits as to which sense-slackening

time has blinded me; or it may have been over-colored by my then over-ardent imaginings, which—a very vast while ago—were over-ready to detect, as Charles Kingsley has put it, in every goose a swan. I do not know.

And that, in passing, is a phrase which I use with timidness. I admit it to be archaic and fallen into desuetude, among in any event all the persons with whom I may pretend, with a pretence which nowadays stays more or less self-conscious, to be familiar.

But for myself, I—nowadays—I derive a pusillanimous, base comfort from saying, "I do not know." And I dare, too, to look back with a shamestruck wondering upon the huge number of years it took me to learn this so comfortable, magic-working and unhuman formula. —For I used to resemble the more sane and wholesome majority of my fellow creatures in that I also once knew everything, or at least in that, but a few decades ago, uncertainty stayed to me, by and large, a stranger.

And my fellow creatures, so do I reflect, they still keep on doing it, to every side of me, alike in social converse, and in their orations (howsoever remote I may observe to be my fellowhood with orators), and in their books, and in their newspapers, and in their state documents, and in their sermons, and in their manifest obligations as a loving wife, and in all yet other arenas of human arrogance, uplifted and well fortified by, so the phrase runs, the courage of their convictions. I alone seem not to be thoroughly and wholly informed as to all affairs concerning politics, and military deployments, and religion, and racial inequalities, and the intentions of Russia, and business conditions, and the unworth of arguing about it any longer (when it is just as plain as the nose on your face) in one's family circle, and vitamins, and the future of communism and of American letters—and in fact, concerning the future of everything else—I alone of a race who, more normally, are gifted with omniscience. It is a reflection which at times depresses me, almost.

Yet I continue to say meekly, as to these and yet many other high matters, "I do not know." And I am thus revolutionary in conduct simply because, if just now and then, I grow over-conscious, nowadays, of not really knowing anything whatever, not with conviction, about any doings anywhere except only that which may, at the moment, be going on inside my own personal and private, if scantily thatched, skull. —Besides which, this eccentric admission saves me a great deal of argument and of trouble in general.

However! the point from which I have diva-
gated (with so very over-much of uncalled-for
and of an egoistic garrulousness, you may well
observe) is but that in youth, or to my experience
of youth, one takes it for granted that the writer
of a printed book speaks with authority and
knows what he is talking about. That which he
tells you as to human life and concerning human
beings the self-conscious inexperience of a youthful reader accepts as veracious. But I am afraid
that should this so remuneratively humble-
minded reader consort a bit later on with writers,
or perhaps even concoct a volume or two himself,
then he and this inestimable faith must part
company, willy-nilly.

He will notice that, in drear point of fact, the
professional writer is apt to know so remarkably
little about *Homo sapiens* (of which mammal I
take him to rank as what the learned in medicine
term a diverticulum) as to be unable to get along
in peace with any other representative of his
species—at close quarters, that is—for more than
a rather brief while.

So very ill indeed does the more highly gifted
writer understand human conditions that well-
nigh always he permits his own private life to
be wrecked by them. He turns to an excess of
alcohol, or of women, or of boys, or of petty
squabbles, almost inevitably. He makes use of

his acquaintances without scruple; he wheedles, and he backbites, unceasingly; and he stays forever, even in his more conscientious and zealous approaches toward sincerity in speech and action, an habitual liar.

He in fine, the more I consider him, leaves me the more content with not being, not any longer, a gifted writer, not after all, with the bright hubbub of my heyday safely survived. He purges me of degraded sentiments, yes, even of envying Francis X. Flubberdub and Gideon Gibberish.

Nor is this catalogue of undesirable vices, I submit, unnatural. All writers, even those who bask in the splendor of a fifteenth reprinting, remain mentally unbalanced, in that they devote their brains to a pursuit for which the human brain, no matter what may have been the first purpose of this dubious gift, was beyond question not designed primarily. They in fine become psychopathic cases; and they, quite properly, tend to behave as such.

In brief, I esteem it the hall mark of a literary genius not ever to sympathize with our human living here, and not ever to arrange with it a satisfying compromise, whether in his personal over-transitory flesh or in print. Rather is it his vocation, his exalted calling—or it may be, his mania—to invent an expurgated and a re-colored

and a generally improved version of life's botch-
eries, a version which he handles with paternal
affection, because he and none other begot this
version; and to communicate to us, at least partially, the delights which he got out of its engen-
dering. He in short induces, if but temporarily, a
collection of high-hearted day-dreams to which,
temporarily, we grant belief.

Now, hereabouts at least, I adhere to logic and
to the main body of all literature's recorded
history. Should you, though, my revered rare
reader, affect the quaint and moonstruck schism
that it ought to be, nowadays, the ignoble practice
of polite letters to dwell upon, and to copy with
a parrot's slavishness, the actual conditions of our
human life, in terms of what the uncontaminated
by reason call "realism," why, then logic will be
demanding of you how does one set to work to
copy the unknown? Logic will be reminding you
that no one of us knows anything whatever except
what happens inside his own skull.

About external matters a writer, in common
with all the rest of us, can but indulge in guess-
work, he of necessity must invent surmises. The
"realist," by and large, prefers degraded and
drab-colored conjectures; it is but a question of
taste, and of his not over-certainly blameworthy
taste, inasmuch as it seems to be shared by
millions; for a vast number of unaccountable

persons appear to enjoy the depressiveness of these "realistic" fancies.

Harking back to the age-privileged pleasures of egotism, and to that host of once delectable writers who no longer absorb me, I remark that even Shakespeare I find, nowadays, to be somewhat futile reading-matter. Here and there I admire the language with a whole heart; but it seems far too often to clothe puerile sentiments, whereas the story of each drama is—almost always, I believe—no less impossible than incoherent; and in fact, downright silly when you reflect that a fair number of Shakespeare's characters are supposed to be men and women. Not even in the unearthly and coincidence-crammed atmosphere familiar to Elizabethan drama, I feel restively, would men and women behave thus abruptly and with so large a flavor of the inconsistent in order to help out the hobbling and incredible plots patched up by Shakespeare.

His editors and his commentators have done their very utmost to make plausible, here to cite but three examples, the behavior of Cordelia toward Lear (at the play's beginning), and of Iago toward Othello, and of Hamlet toward Ophelia; yet the fact remains that, in each instance, this behavior stays unaccountable. It promotes dramatic action beyond question; but

it likewise flouts common-sense with no less of
completeness than it derides comprehension.

Moreover do I find the people of Shakespeare's
creating to be a trifle over-zealous in their shared
faith that, at all costs in the way of probability or
of human nature, everything requires to be dis-
posed of within five acts. (I mean, of course, as
his plays are printed, with their artificial division
into five acts, a division unknown to Shakespeare
in their performance.) And so when once any
fifth act whatever gets fairly under way, why,
then somebody or other (and well-nigh completely irrespective of his or of her previous conduct and supposed nature) needs all of a sudden
to repent, or to kill somebody else, or to indulge
either in matrimony or suicide, or to put an end
to disguise, or to reveal an important secret,
whichsoever proceeding may tend most quickly
to wind up the plot in which the dramatis personæ
have been implicated. It is almost as though the
actors themselves had decided the performance
to be nonsensical and were eager to be rid of it.

So at any rate do Shakespeare's fifth acts appear
to me. And here no doubt I am wrong.

Meanwhile, I in any case am not attempting to
belittle Shakespeare, but merely to expound, and
at need to expose, myself, as I have become under
the pilferings of senescence. I find that I do not
any longer, no, not very much, delight in reading

the text of earth's concededly supreme author.

§8. IN FACT, it is my present-day belief that all
dramatists afford lean reading-matter. —For it
seems to me that a writer is, or that at least now
and then some more improvident writer attempts
to be, an artist whose medium is the written word;
whereas the concern of a dramatist with the
written word is minor. The dramatist, whose
medium is an undescribable mélange of human
bodies and of colored lights and of movement and
of paint and of fanciful apparel and of music and
of mob psychology, all more or less skillfully
blended with spoken dialogue, is not in any
generic sense, to my finding, a writer.

And I now and then wonder if, in the dawn of
some highly improbable and more rational day,
our entire approach to literature might not be re-
organized advantageously out of deference to this
truism? It would very much help matters; for as
yet the approved libraries of all countries remain
cluttered up with the printed plays of dramatists
who were excellent dramatists. Their connection
with adroit and well rounded-off literary art, however, stays depressingly infrequent.

So one still hears, of course, that the main glory
of English literature is revealed, with an eternal
steadfastness, in the plays of William Shakespeare. Here, to my finding, is still another tarra-

diddle which we may not ever look to see discredited. Yet I likewise believe any fairly honest person will admit, just in private, that the plays of Shakespeare, when approached as reading-matter, are rather remarkably makeshift reading-matter. They display commendable patches of lyric sweetness and of orotund rhetoric, I repeat; and these still delight the judicious; but, in the actors' absence, one finds, nowadays, a host of ever-present and regrettably crude, harsh gaps.

Thus Shakespeare, when in his proper station behind the footlights, proves opulent in fine death scenes such as are but a very little less tragic than the usual results of a Presidential election; and all these, when you read them, dwindle to a laconic "[*Dies.*" I shall not dwell upon the droll way in which this chill-blooded and flippant parenthesis runs through the last scene of *The Tragical History of Hamlet, Prince of Denmark,* like the refrain of a song, of an awkwardly comic song. I select a far fairer test. I suggest that this "[*Dies*" really does appear, in the reading of it, a cavalier fashion in which to dismiss ruined Lear; and that Thackeray, for an instance, did not thus curtly dispose of Lieutenant-Colonel Thomas Newcome, once of the Bengal Cavalry, but later identified with the Bundlecund Banking Company.

Thackeray, in brief, was a writer where Shakespeare stayed a dramatist, each dealing masterfully with his medium and each honoring nobly the obligations of his medium. It was a part of Thackeray's task to kill off his elderly Colonel with a befitting efficientness, in the way of verbal scenery and of auctorial reflections, along with an opportune chapel bell and a pleasing ascension into heaven; whereas Shakespeare needed to entrust his elderly King's dissolution to Richard Burbage and a monosyllable.

It was sound dramatic policy. My point is merely that the following out of this policy has here resulted in maimed and poverty-stricken reading-matter. And for no instant would I present this fact, do you let me repeat, as a depreciation of Shakespeare, whose *True Chronicle History of the Life and Death of King Lear and His Three Daughters* was never meant to become reading-matter. Shakespeare, as an appreciative student and a gifted plagiarist of literature, appears to have done his very utmost to prevent his plays from being rehashed, and of necessity misrepresented, in book form. He was foiled, it is true, by larcenous shorthand writers, abetted by that greedy indiscretion which seems to attack the executors of every distinguished author; yet none the less ought we to honor his intentions with applause.

Meanwhile: when these plays are acted, the most of them still serve superbly the ends for

which they were designed. The self-contradic-
tions of the play's story and its childish anachro-
nisms, no less in conduct than in speech, and its
snapshot summaries remain disturbing factors in
the more leisured, in the more mature, and in the
far wider field of literature. But within the dramatist's allotted two hours or thereabouts of time,
and upon the dramatist's inelastic stage, they now
and then become necessities.

Moreover, these incongruities are exceedingly
well hidden by the circumstance that you do, as
a matter of unarguable fact, perceive the play's
extravagant action to be performed by quite un-
mistakable human beings. You can no longer
object, with Ibsen's Judge Brack, that "People
don't do such things," when before your eyes and
beyond any disputation, people all seriously and
actually are doing such things.

Both incredulity and reason are thus temporarily drugged by the evidence of your own
senses, when you are witnessing, let us say, a
performance of *Twelfth Night*. Why—you may
well wonder half-vexedly when reading *Twelfth
Night; or, What You Will* in your library—but
why, in high heaven's name, should Viola disguise
herself as a castrato, or in fact, why disguise herself at all? and why should Olivia then become
bent upon marrying the supposed eunuch? The
entire affair seems nonsense.

But upon the stage you note with approval that a tolerably well built young woman is affording you an agreeable opportunity to admire her figure. You are then not especially perplexed that Olivia should share in your admiration. It proves, rather, her good taste. —For the dramatist yet again has beguiled you with yet another adroit use of his medium, a medium which beyond discreet pubic limits includes human anatomy.

My point is merely that, in the main, this medium is not literature. The mimic moribundities of a gifted tragedian or the plump legs of a leading lady may display innumerous merits; but no one of them is literary. My point is that an actually good play, by the very virtue of what makes for efficiency when it is acted, becomes a partially dead product when it is being read; and that this persistent, this pig-headed attempt to convert drama into reading-matter has overcrowded our bookshelves with paralytics. I take the printed plays of Shakespeare to be among such paralytics, yes, even in the same breath that I praise God for having created William Shakespeare.

§9. AT LEAST, I SUPPOSE I DO THANK GOD FOR William Shakespeare, with an indefinite cordiality.

I am grateful for Shakespeare, in fine, somewhat as I nowadays render heavenward my uncertain, tentative thanks for an as yet unimpaired liver; and for the droll dearness of that peremptory person to whom, how all incredibly, I am now married; and for the beauty of moonlit nights; and for the continuance, in howsoever qualified a degree, of my sexual desires; and for the possibilities of English prose; and for the elations of alcohol; and for my memories of divers once amiable and adored long-perished women; and for the wistfulness of sunsets; and for the savor of

REGARDS
CONTENTMENT
IN
COMPROMISE

poached eggs; and for the so impressively multitudinary horde of my books, books which were not anywhere before I created them; and for yet a many other miscellaneous amenities of my current quiet living.

—For about God, I find, I do not often think nowadays, either one way or another, except only with this constant but vague sense of gratitude for His past and present favors, in the event of His indeed being somewhere upstairs.

I can recall, with an exceeding clearness, just how I used to think about Him during the earlier eighteen-eighties, as an elderly Jewish gentleman, addicted to wearing dressing-gowns, Who after the Crucifixion had joined the Catholic Church, and later had become an Episcopalian. And all that seemed natural enough, inasmuch as in Richmond every one of the Jewish families about whom you knew anything, and whose existence was recognized by the upper classes of Richmond, had become Episcopalians not any great while before your time.

You could understand about God's having a son also, even if it did seem sort of curious that God's wife was already married to somebody else. Probably she had just got a divorce like some ladies did. Anyhow, you could understand about Christ pretty well, although at this period it was with an uneasy feeling of not really liking him, not exactly. You ought to, you knew. Still, you felt that he and you would not ever have got along together, no, not exactly, upon account of his being, well, sort of too good all the time and his preaching so much. There in fact was one of your mother's own cousins who did every one of these repellent things; and you just simply couldn't stand having him around.

So it was only about the Holy Ghost that you wondered when you were as yet in short trousers, because you could not at all understand what this nebulous figure had to do with anything else. He was up there in heaven, though, along with your Grandfather Branch and your Grandmother Cabell, and you had not ever seen them either. So in church it was right for everybody to say, every Sunday morning, that you believed Jesus Christ was conceived by this Holy Ghost, whatever in the world that might mean.

I am afraid that now I have attained to the maturity which the uncivil term old age, my religious convictions are not two whits, or even one single individual whit, more clear cut than they were in my childhood. I have remained an Episcopalian, accepting incuriously the doctrines of my church (to the limited extent that I could find them comprehensible) as being true, for anything which I knew to the contrary. I still do not see any difficulty in believing that God exists, although not of necessity in a dressing gown designed by Gustave Doré.

I cannot imagine, though, this God's being at all interested in my beliefs, either one way or another. Nor can I imagine His being at pains to keep an exact record of my sins and misdeeds. And in any case, I reflect resignedly, His nature and His tastes and His daily, and in particular His nocturnal, supervision of mankind are matters very far beyond my control. If ever these divine qualities and avocations should be revealed to me, I shall have to accept them as I best can. I consider them as yet to be none of my business.

Meanwhile, though, I prefer to believe in His existence in order that I may be grateful to Him. He gave me, so do I prefer to think, where an opinion stays untrammeled, the mind and the body from which I have derived a vast deal of enjoyment, by and large, throughout more than seventy years. He gave me—perhaps, at any rate —the common pleasures of life, the pleasures which are offered to everybody; and I remember them as a sufficing ground for warm gratitude. In short, I plead guilty to having enjoyed—still, by and large—my longer than usual living here upon earth. And I needs render thanks for it, to Somebody.

Moreover, through this God's at any rate not impossible indulgence, I have been permitted to do what I most wanted to do, which was to write my now disregarded and obsolete and, in consequence, all-hurtless books.

I long ago, in common with my nearer and more candid relatives, gave up guessing at why I needed to write books, that problem which nowadays so very many of my reviewers also dismiss loftily, as being without any conceivable solution.

I know only that since I was sixteen or there-abouts, I have had this wish to be writing; and that the indulgence of this wish has proved to me a singular pleasure.

In most cases I have desired to see published that which I wrote; and as befitted my Scots ancestry, I have desired to be paid for my writing as much money as I could extort from its publishers, those not over-prodigal accountants. These two desires, and especially the latter one, still seem to me comprehensible, nay, even rational.

To the other side, I beyond doubt did write so very incredibly much without any special expectancy of its publication, during the first eighteen years which I devoted to failing at authorship; and I have been guilty of an intolerable amount of both verse and prose to the printing of which I upon no terms would ever have consented. Such conduct seems to me far from rational; I cannot explain it; I know only that I have enjoyed the interminable and finicky labor of doing so much writing, which later on I typed, and then retyped, with zest, even though I was planning, when once its vocabulary and its cadences and its sentence structures and its prose feet and its other verbal kickshaws had been tinkered with enough to content me, to destroy every line of it.

The main drawback to this pursuit of writing as a virtually sensuous form of self-indulgence, as a sort of drug-taking, so do I concede nowadays, is that it has prevented me from earning any considerable amount of money. During the last fifty years, I reflect, I (with my so wide and my so widely squandered opportunities), why, but even I might how far more thriftily have appraised each current trend of literature—or at any rate, of reading-matter—and I might have written so as to conform with the spring or the autumn vogue, or even with the mental declivities of the American Academy of Arts and Letters, perhaps, if only I had not found any such intelligent behavior to be, for my limited talents, a physical impossibility.

Always I have been able to write only that which at the time I desired to write, whether it were a legend or a short story or a bit of archaic verse or a one-act drama or a novel or a dirty limerick or a flagrant romance or a dialogue or a river's history or an essay or an intimate letter to some deceased personage or even a dry-as-dust genealogical book. If I attempted to write about anything else than what for the moment had snared my fancy, then almost instantly I found myself unable to write at all.

How woefully much time, too (does my conscience remind me), have I squandered in diverting myself with a multitude of English prose styles! And I concede meekly that year-long wastefulness, making only the tacit yet defiant reservation that I derived from it pleasure, an ever unfailing placid enjoyment. —So that I ought in consequence (logic whispers) to be as grateful to my own books as I am to those of Sir Walter Scott and William Harrison Ainsworth, upon very much the same grounds and with an equal distaste for reading them.

Now, if hereabouts I make bold to confess that in my time I have wantoned through a not narrow range of styles, it is merely because of my desire, esteemed reader, to share with you alone a secret which nobody else appears to have detected.

As I have remarked in another place, whensoever since 1920 I have published a book it has evoked always the same brace of reviews—the one of which regretted that here was *Jurgen* all over again, whereas the other deplored that my latest literary indiscretion was by no means another *Jurgen*. Yet even these inveterate acquaintances do not often fail to comment upon my "style," as a sort of staple commodity, or, so let us put it, as a verbarian Worcestershire Sauce which lends to everything its own distinctive and uniform, unvarying flavor, such as you may or may not like, but cannot mistake for anything else.

To this sole end (upon all such occasions do I

reflect guiltily) have I adapted and blended one with another—in varying proportions, self-consciously and pharmaceutically, with a meticulous preciseness—the literary manner and the phrasing and the sentence building of scores upon scores of authors, selecting always those two or three or perhaps yet more writers who for my book's purpose seemed best imitable, to the sole end that these piddling labors should half-drug and content me, selfishly, in a cloistered privateness.

And nobody ever caught me at these nefarious, so multiform alchemies; or at least, nobody of large prominence has been at pains to expose me. The majority of virtuosi have continued to print commentaries—and for the most part, not uncivil commentaries, I dare boast—upon that staple commodity, my "style," that "style" which, developing with *The Eagle's Shadow* in 1904, has prevailed steadfastly and unchanged throughout some fifty books, yes, even down to *The Devil's Own Dear Son* in 1949, so should I infer.

—Only, I don't infer anything of the sort. My deductions have ranged quite otherwhither, with an impenitent thankfulness, toward that time-wasting of which I enjoyed every moment.

§10. WELL, but it follows that in the teeth of a half-century's unarguable and all-profitless hedonism, I dare not affect any highminded indignation over the how far more rational practice of so far "prostituting one's art" as to write, more or less candidly, that particular sort of balderdash which "the reading public," or which some special magazine editor, may at the instant be buying with avidity. I likewise would have followed this sane businesslike course, and with a laudable oftenness, I assure my rebuking conscience, if only I had ever been able to.

—For nowadays (and it skills not what I may have thought yesterday), nowadays common-sense bids me perceive nothing at all unpraise-worthy in the manufacture of such sleazy and impermanent reading-matter, not any more than I would contemn a reporter upon the staff of my morning paper, nor any more than I would raise a lament over the manufacture of chewing gum or of contraceptives or of motor cars. A popular need is being supplied, harmlessly and with financial profit; that is all, so does common-sense assure me.

Nor does common-sense find it to the purpose, not nowadays, that the writer who is turning out such lucrative pishposh may be capable of writing with more dignity and more art and more urbane-ness and more truth, and in brief, of contributing his or her quota by-and-by to that astounding hodgepodge which we describe as American lit-erature. To be ranked as an American classic,

along with James Fenimore Cooper and with John
Greenleaf Whittier and with the James brothers
(but not as a co-equal in ever-living legendry with
Frank James and Jesse James, of course) and with
Henry Wadsworth Longfellow and with Walt
Whitman and with William Dean Howells and
with Willa Cather—or perhaps even along with
the Swedishly admired Mr. William Faulkner and
Mrs. Pearl Buck—appears to be somewhat com-
promising, says common-sense.

And besides that (says charity), most writers
need to consider their indebtedness to the land-
lord and to the local liquor store and to the local
grocer and to a wife or so, in the form of overdue
alimony, and to the local Collector of Internal
Revenue, and to their yet other legal obligations
in general, as befits a good citizen, before they
can find enough time in which to consider their
indebtedness to an, after all, remote and problem-
atic and a less over-urgent posterity.

Nor of course has posterity ever done anything
for their benefit—or for your benefit or for my
benefit or for anybody's benefit—such as would
establish an indebtedness. Here is a truism which
reason tends to neglect, and most orators to defy.
Common-sense assures us, however, there is no
sane motive for writers to be bothering about
posterity. We instead ought to profit, so does

common-sense tell us, by observing the remunerative forthrightness of our better statesmen, who,
without any too much unseemly boasting as to
their acumen, concede always the unimportance
of posterity's verdict upon their babbled imbecili-
ties and frank skulduggery—or for that matter,
the unimportance of posterity's annihilation—as
compared with the results of an oncoming
election.

So common-sense tells us, I repeat; but I need
to repeat also that I nowadays have come to
esteem with a marked distrust the upshot of
common-sense and of man's rationality and of
human logic. I very much regard as being more
vital our human dreams, our requisite endless
illusions, which defy common-sense; and of some
of these I have spoken, alike in this book and in
all my other books.

Yet I do not mean merely those so useful tarradiddles with which the prisoner in every human
skull must bedrug his captivity. I refer, now, to
those how far more noble fictions such as we have
all known; such as demolish the fetters of logic
overnight; and such as, at least now and then,
escort each of us away from his legal post office
address into this or the other resplendent kingdom beyond common-sense. I mean, in a word,
those high adventures which some of us at any
rate are privileged to encounter during that

superior one-third part of our living which is given over to sleep.

That is why I once wrote an entire trilogy as to just one of these commonplace, superb fortuities, a performance upon which I am now moved to comment, in chief because nobody anywhere appeared to understand whatever in this world I could imagine I was driving at when I published those three books throughout all which my protagonist, that so easily identified Virginian writer, stayed sound asleep.

With your permission, O tenacious reader who have struggled on thus far amid my digressions, I shall now explain why.

§11. TO BEGIN WITH A COGENT TRUISM, THROUGH sleep only may we attain an existence not over troubled by weariness; and of tedium also may sleep rid us by unbarring new worlds.

Yet furthermore: sleep may create a magnanimity such as, under the present tax system, we cannot afford during our waking hours, inasmuch as sleep, like the authentic geniuses of literature to whom I have referred earlier, not infrequently produces high-hearted dreams in which even the most watery-spirited of us are permitted to live without forethought—faring hand and glove, as it were, with the miraculous and the fervent and the heroic, now that, for a glad interregnum, Time and Time's stolid offspring, whom we name Common-Sense, have abated their tyrannies.

CONSIDERS
ONE-THIRD
OF
OUR LIVING

—For in dreamland one lives unchronologically. The squandered past is revived, along with its most noble and lovely dead, that superior race who flourished when we first began shaving; and now they are no longer estranged, but they become all-forgiving when we reveal to them, with an unchecked and surprising eloquence, that which our prudence, or our youth's bashfulness,

or it may be our duty, had forbidden. They listen
fondly, even with some traces of reverence, now
that in dreamland our nearer kindred and our
lost loves appreciate for the first time our superb
qualities fully.

And besides that, a number of slight, tattered,
debonair illusions escape from out of the barred
future, like elfin jail-breakers, in the form of our
hopes for tomorrow, all realized unlastingly
through sleep's magic; and the rogues set about
their nocturnal felonies by bribing off the day's
bitterness or defeat with frail fairy gold, and by
hiring with the same international currency an
assassin for every daylit trouble.

It is true that some persons, every once in a
while, sleep with less splendor; and are at pains
to find misery even in dreamland. But you and I,
let us hope, have not been tutored over often, by
inclement experience, to sympathize with be-
nighted beings who display any such unwisdom.

So then, let it be repeated, may we fare hand
and glove with the miraculous and the fervent
and the heroic; and everything seems high-
hearted, all is quite pleasant, while the dream
lasts. But morning (as rather possibly you may
have noticed) dispels every one of these agree-
abilities, posthaste, with a petulant chirping of
half-awakened birds or, in more urban circumstances, with the sedate hoof-beats of the local

milk wagon. Time and Common-Sense return to us depressingly, now that yet again they establish over prostrate and still imbedded mankind their drab sovereignty. And to the untrammeled and ardent, glad, flashing melée of dreamland the two of them speak in unison, with the smug authority of a registered nurse, saying,—

"Quiet, please."

§12. THEREAFTER, for some sixteen relatively unimportant hours, we must put aside our dreams. Though indeed it is a bit vaingloriously—plain reason should protest at this point—that we make bold to describe any one of these dreams as "ours."

A sleeping tax-payer, to the best of my personal experience, goes into dreamland as an improved and aggrandized version of his everyday self. He becomes a creature very little resembling his wife's major disappointment in life now that sleep has graced him with new powers, with new and hitherto unparalleled turns of speech, with a new intrepidity, and with new turns of reason; for your personality in a dream, should you but reflect upon this matter, is not at all your more humdrum daylit personality.

Through sleep's gracious editing, you become no less different from the person who lies in your bed than are your fine comrades in dreamland. It is thus, by all mundane rules, not really "you" that hold traffic with the affairs of a dream. These somnial transactions do not involve the terrestial "you" one way or the other; and so, by no sound logician, could be described as "yours."

—Which is nonsense, you will remark. And I agree with you. That is just my contention. My point—nay, my truism—is that, logic or no logic, we do know, indissuadably, that our dreams are indeed ours, and are ours also in a sense more dear and more deep than ever can be the enforced compromises of our flesh-and-blood living.

Now, this is a pure heritage of instinctive knowledge (submits the truly sound logician) from which one is compelled to infer that in dreamland we become our true selves, those selves of whom our workaday namesakes remain a cramped parody. And it shows also (the aforesaid, rare, acute logician will go on to educe) that in dreams alone do we actually exist. We do not live, in any at all adequate sense of that verb (will be his continuance), until after the pounds of raw meat which we infest during the daytime have been huddled abed. Furthermore (thus he will perorate, looking toward us nocturnal demigods with some unavoidable admiration), we deserve an historian who will treat of our superhuman everynight exploits with an unstinted, a fearless and a befitting veracity.

That is my second point.

§13. BECAUSE OF THESE TWO POINTS, AND OF SUCH truisms as I have listed, did I attempt, in the trilogy which is called *The Nightmare Has Triplets*, to extend into mature nocturnal dreaming the straightforward naturalism of Lewis Carroll. To acknowledge this high-handed plagiarizing, or rather, to proclaim this discipleship, seems a performance demanded by honesty; and it appears likewise to demand a paragraph or so to explain its meaning.

As far back as in 1929, then, during the revising of *The Cream of the Jest* into its definitive version, the thought came to the author of *The Cream of the Jest* that, with one all-exceptional exception, no American or British author had produced a dream-story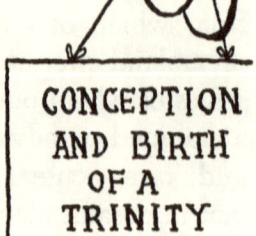

CONCEPTION
AND BIRTH
OF A
TRINITY

combining any considerable length with any considerable pretence to veracity. Here and there you found a brief tale which, in its stinted way, stayed authentic enough. Even in *The Cream of the Jest* you noted, among forty chapters, four chapters which seemed veracious. But Lewis Carroll alone of English writers had made books which dealt, and which dealt only, with the true stuff of dreams; which covered with completeness

the course of a normal dream; and which at every
instant progressed at the pace and after the
manner of a dream, under the fixed local regula-
tions of dreamland.

In *The Cream of the Jest* you considered a
novel builded about the dreams of a romance
writer. But you considered also the real issue
dodged, and dodged doubly, by the facts: (*a*)
that the dreams of Felix Kennaston, as you had
chosen here to call the obsessed author about
whom you thought most often, were indicated by
extracts or summaries; and (*b*) that these dreams
were induced by extraneous means, perhaps, even
though you believed them not to be, magical.
Turning to *The High Place*, to *Jurgen*, to *Figures
of Earth*, and to yet other volumes emergent at
various times from your age-worsened Oliver
Number Nine Typewriter, you considered dreams
which beyond question had been caused by this
or the other intervening magic; and which (in
consequence of four grim reasons that are known
to all students of goetia) must conform to the
logic, and to the touchstones, of a person who is
awake.

None of these volumes recorded any dream
from the authentic, the wholly familiar, stand-
point of an everynight dreamer. And your conscience remarked tactlessly that, after so much
yearlong traffic with dreams, the author of the

Biography of the Life of Manuel had not ever once dealt, not thoroughly, with a normal nocturnal dream—as distinguished, I mean, from those yet other brave illusions such as keep daylight endurable for mankind at large.

§14. STILL more odd seemed the fact that, when you came to think of it, there did not appear to exist in American prose literature, whether in its maturity or during its more gracious childhood in England, any full-length dream-story which obeyed the actual and well-known laws of a normal dream—with the ever-memorable exception of the two Alice books by Lewis Carroll. These books alone did preserve the peculiar, the unremittent movement of a normal dream, and its peculiar logic, and its peculiar legerdemain, through which the people one meets or the places visited, in a normal dream, are enabled unostentatiously to take form or to vanish without provoking in the beholder's mind any flavor of surprise; just as these books preserved, too, the so often present knowledge, common to most dreamers, that, after all, one is dreaming.

But I forbear to particularize the true somnial touch with which matters are handled by Lewis Carroll. My point here is that, in 1929 at least, these two books about Alice and her tours of dreamland appeared inexplicably unfellowed in

English, as the sole known examples, by and large, of a constant and unflinching naturalism applied to the lands beyond common-sense.

Even so, the oneirocritic needs to file an objection. Alice smells pepper in Wonderland; she smells the "scented rushes" in Looking-Glass Land; and upon several occasions Alice partakes of food and of physic also—reducing needfully her size almost at outset, as you will remember, by means of an unusual medicine which had "a sort of mixed flavor of cherry-tart, custard, pineapple, roast turkey and hot buttered toast."

Such fantasies grieve the judicious. But the precisian they madden, because throughout every land beyond common-sense into which human beings have as yet entered, it is a known rule that in no dream, unless it be induced by black magic or gray magic, may a dreaming person ever taste or smell anything. So this dual, not unflagrant exception to the scientific exactitude of Lewis Carroll needs here to be recorded—with the supplement, the glad supplement, that in every other important respect one finds these two Alice books to be triumphs in naturalism with which the most admired novels of George Moore, or of Zola, or of Dreiser, let us say, cannot be compared, not very profitably.

§15. RETURNING to *The Cream of the Jest*, it seemed increasingly needful to the author of *The Cream of the Jest*, during the squandered but delighted-in months which he gave over to revising *The Cream of the Jest*, that some soothsayer other than Lewis Carroll should narrate a full-length dream, at full length, realistically. One means, of course, that in depicting for our admonishment the ugly and gloom-ridden and sex-obsessed monstrosity which a defection in the frivolous labels "the truth" as to man's life during his wide-awake hours, our professed realists at all times had restricted their tediousness to a mere two-thirds of mankind's existence—without ever presuming, it would seem, to venture beyond that rather vulgar fraction. Every one of their novels displayed a cowed subjection to insomnia.

The eight hours, more or less, which mankind in general devote to sleep appeared to repel the professed realist; to disgust him, perhaps, as being hours which were too light-minded to respect his formula for "the truth"; and in short, to be a theme which he dared not handle. Dreams had been analyzed and interpreted, *ad*, as the learned say, *infinitum*, and even, as the impatient append, *ad nauseam*; but never since 1871 had any British or American writer dealt with any convincing, complete dream completely and convincingly.

All this, too, in face of the plain fact that most

persons spend one-third of their lifetimes in sleep, during which (according at least to such eminent authorities as Kant, Leibnitz, Descartes, and yet other reputable philosophers) every sleeper dreams continuously; and so lives, for some eight hours out of each twenty-four hours, among un-terrestial surroundings, and exercises unearthly powers. Yet Lewis Carroll alone of our better-known realists had dug in this huge field, this entire third of human life, with the spade of sincerity. And even this great pioneer had con-fined his labors to the south temperate zone, as it were, in the callow and sexless dreams of a child.

It followed that nowhere in English prose liter-ature was an adult dream depicted with realism; and that some thirty-three per cent of human ex-perience remain unrepresented, at all truthfully. Since John Bunyan's time there had been an abundance of prose volumes which purported to record dreams; but, in English at least, only two such books had tried honestly to respect the con-ditions of dreamland, that world in which all tolerably wholesome persons pass a third of their lives.

It really did seem a default which ought to be remedied.

§16. HERE, in *The Cream of the Jest*, glimmered a fair starting point for that remedying. Only, of course, my protagonist must not be a professional writer, because caution whispered that in yet another volume to present the dreamer as one who lived wastefully during his waking hours, by devoting them to the production of books which were not balderdash, would make it difficult for the obtuse to see in the result anything except a revamping of *The Cream of the Jest.*

My protagonist could as easily be a musician or a painter, said caution; though indeed, for that matter, without any large difficulty he could be made a stock broker, or a minister of the Christian gospel (a notion with some fine possibilities), or a merchant, or an attorney, or even more simply, a person of independent means and leisure. Such persons were remarkably plentiful during the far-away first half of 1929, when I was visited by these reflections, a good while before each and everybody's income became a donation to the federal government.

In brief, the main needs of my protagonist, as the tale shiftingly took form to the back of my thoughts, seemed to be a fair allowance of literacy and of imagination, and of his own theories about creative art, and of loquaciousness also.

But if—as experience forthwith assured me— but if I did make my protagonist a professional writer, then instantly my original would be suspect. No dullard anywhere would be able,

quite, to avoid the belief that, yet again, I was
writing about myself; and as a further, not un-
salutary consequence, no dullard would fail to be
rather cordially irritated. It is for this reason, do
you let me remark in passing, that so very often
I have inclined to make of my protagonist a
writer, or at least a potential writer; and have
labored toward the same goal through the hy-
phenation of Richmond-in-Virginia.

To this effect did experience woo me, outwhis-
pering caution; and sturdily prompting me not to
remit the pleasures promised by a continuance in
what the obtuse might reprove as egotism. —For
as I have explained to you previously, all truthful
writing has to be egotism. Well, but it followed
that, inasmuch as any graying house-holder in
Philistia who has reached middle-life knows experience to be the best teacher, so then to the in-
sistent voice of experience I hearkened, meltingly.

I in short decided that my protagonist might
most pleasurably be made an author with all such
loquacious tendencies as married life has taught
me to admire mutely. Yet furthermore I would
introduce an odd touch of novelty by depicting
him as a Virginian, because not ever before had
I written a story about a Virginian.

—Whereafter this Virginian writer began to
solidify, a little by a little, during his slow emer-
gence from out of that shadowy realm in which

the as yet uncreated characters of fiction abide restively; and his traits took form. He in this manner became the Peripatetic Episcopalian, that unparalleled quintessence of the Commonwealth of Virginia's patrician culture; and he revealed to me that Smirt and Smith and Smire were his triple names, his inevitable epithets, his *mots justes.* After that, he began to reveal also the varied incidents of his long dreaming just as clearly as, but not a jot more clearly than, they had been revealed to him.

§ 17. HE REVEALED LIKEWISE, THERE IS NO DENYING, when I came to convert his dreaming into words and sentences and punctuation marks, the unpliant obstinacy of a well-born Virginian.

"But that," he would repeat, parrot-like, whensoever I attempted to touch up a bit improvingly his revealings, "that is not the way it was."

And there was no doing anything whatever with the man until I had returned meekly to his how far less attractive version of the affair in hand. He in this fashion caused me persistent trouble through what seemed to me his over insistence upon uninvention and the unornamented, the barely actual happening.

ATTENDS
ON THE
SUBLIME
VIRGINIAN

Nevertheless, from such word-of-mouth materials I managed to begin the record of his dreaming, in *Smirt*; and so, during the first book about the Peripatetic Episcopalian, I followed my protagonist out of Richmond-in-Virginia, through a small, cobweb-covered gate of horn, even until we had reached that happy planet (which, one of its astronomers informed me later on, is a not large satellite of Beta Centauri) destined to be re-organized by Smirt's literary influence during the while that he played at being god.

A number of matters were thus changed fun-
damentally when I began work upon *Smith;* huge
difficulties had been made lighter; and my progress henceforward became facile. —For need I
explain that, after I had once got into the planet
which the Seven Stewards remodelled under my
illustrious and urbane friend's benign supervision,
I was not any longer dependent upon what he
chose, or what he declined, to communicate, now
that to me likewise these special lands beyond
common-sense had been laid open?

The question is rhetorical. None might answer
my question, revered reader, without presup-
posing your complete lack of intelligence; and to
wanton in any such incivility is beyond the orbit
of my purpose. That rare discernment which has
led you to borrow or perhaps even to purchase
this book will assure you that I could now appraise
the bright flanks, the faëry seas, the magic-
haunted continents, the fabulous kingdoms, and
the resplendent contents in general of my friend's
remodelled planet, not merely by the reports—
how unavoidably biased!—of its bland demiurge,
but through the unaided aid of my own faculties,
when once I had been allowed to enter these
dream-engendered places, and through my own
spectacles to behold them, as under Smirt's dor-
mant influence they had been reformed and made
populous.

I could get now, at first hand, a reliable medley of information from the inhabitants of each one of these lands beyond common-sense. What was far more important, as went my immediate needs, I could likewise consult their traditions, their folk-lore, their scholastic tomes, and their theological speculations, as to their but partially credible, anthropomorphic Creator: it having been permitted me in this way to amplify my history of the sublime Virginian's exploits after Smirt became Lord of the Forest, as Mr. Smith.

§18. ONE remained, to be sure, in my friend's dreaming, of which all these matters were by-products—but with the large difference that, like most great literary artists, he had set in action, and he had builded so permanently as to outlast his own powers, a world which still had its existence; and through the by-paths of which he who at one time had been its Supreme Being must tread nowadays, somewhat furtively, as a mere demigod, not unsuspiciously regarded, now that the glories of Mr. Smith (like those of yet another so easily identified Virginian author, it of course occurred to me) were no longer predominant.

And besides that, my fallen friend, in his role as Lord of the Forest, at first seemed to be dreaming, a whit discursively, about events in which he himself had no share. Such conduct puzzled me

not a little when I began to write out the second
book of the epic of the Peripatetic Episcopalian.

Then by-and-by I untangled the enigma. I saw,
as, apparently, the Lord of the Forest did not
ever see, that the four sons whom he fetched to
his sylvan kingdom were merely as many aspects
of himself. During the period of his omnipotence
in the heaven which was called Amit he had per-
sonified his own stubborn wilfulness, his own
blind self-complacency, his own inveterate poet-
icizing, and his own pig-headed pedantry, in those
four of his offspring whom, severally, he had
elected to name Volmar, and Elair, and Clitandre,
and Little Smirt.

In this manner did he who had played at being
god now play at being the son of god. And each
one of these four children I now noted to be, at
bottom—like Manuel, and like Jurgen, and like
Florian de Puysange—a distorted copy of their
not unadmiring begetter, with one special feature
especially emphasized.

In fine this Supreme Being had honored the
customary divine routine by creating men in his
own image. So did it still remain true that, as in
Poictesme, and as Smirt himself had observed
during the genesis of his privately owned planet
(in place of a mere province), "everywhither
rode abridged likenesses of Smirt upon magnifi-
cent quests; and each one of these secondary

Smirts was speaking the most polished diction, and was doing any number of impossible things, in the lands beyond common-sense."

And so likewise did I perceive that the all-gifted Virginian whose dreaming I commemorated was still dreaming about his own high doings and about his own applaudability, under this or the other alias. The accustomed dietary of his egoism was being reflavored with a new sauce. Such was the sole altering—here as in Poictesme, or, for that matter, in Lichfield. The man was still thinking about the only person as to whom he knew anything whatever with assurance.

When I came to record, in *Smire*, the third and the final phase of his dreaming, wherein my protagonist became a not over-prudishly holy ghost, why, but then I continued, with that fidelity which scientific research demands at all times of its practitioner, to avail myself of the annals of these special lands beyond common-sense—the lands created by my fellow Virginian—during the while that I completed this chronicle of the decreed progress which is made by every Supreme Being toward oblivion, when once to his nation-wide famousness, and to all the high laudations of his postulants (even as to mine, I of course reflected), Time has remarked austerely,—

"Quiet, please."

And I tried also to satisfy my curiosity as to the somewhat important problem, What is the status of humankind during that third of our existence which we pass in dreamland?

It is a question, I found, to which the philosophers, a number of scientists, and indeed one or two of the more liberal politicians, of the lands beyond common-sense, have devoted a not inconsiderable amount of study, upon the off-chance that mankind in some way or another might be made useful. Yet have these various students of anthropology labored without reaching any general agreement. By one school of philosophy—by the Rationalists, alike in Druim and Achren—it is held that mankind must necessarily be a by-product of the more implausible and perturbed dreams of the people of dreamland, inasmuch as the recorded history and the current doings of our race (which these Rationalists as yet study nightly with an amazed interest) are simply not possible. And to that contention, of course, no reply can be made within the narrow fields of pure reason.

Nevertheless, there are not lacking in dreamland those outmoded mystics who to every sort of merely rational argument answer, *Credo quia impossible est*. And this minority as yet clings— in diminishing numbers, I grant you—to their begetters' old human faith that, in spite of logic, and just as the rustic tribes of Branlon relate, men and women do truly exist; and that, over and over again, it is permitted to these fantastic and frail, flesh-and-blood monsters to haunt visibly the lands beyond common-sense.

In brief, the question may be described as technically open, so far as the peoples of dreamland are concerned; but their faith in mankind remains at best an obsolescent and a concededly far-fetched hypothesis.

§19. I MUST RECORD HERE THE REGRET OF THIS great Virginian that, throughout the course of his dreaming, he was subject to the restrictions which, I believe, govern all our nocturnal dreams. Thus, he lacked not merely the ability to smell or to taste anything. His powers of vision also were circumscribed, indescribably.

Why, but yes, he explained to me, after his earthly landing at the mouth of the Potomac River, upon the beach before Poynton Lodge, oh, yes, you could see everything clearly enough, so far as went practical needs. It was only that a sort of mistiness pervaded all dreamland, driftingly and unpredictably. And besides that, at times, one or another visual detail would seize on your attention, obsessing it,

AS TO
SEVERAL LAWS
OF
DREAMLAND

somewhat as if, from the indefinite mistings which were like an all-shrouding yet very thin fog, this particular detail—a white eyebrow, it might be, or a red notebook possibly, or the sleek black-bordered face of a clock, or perhaps the steel tip of a spear or the soiled crease in a purple tunic—had been picked out by a flashlight. In consequence, you did not ever obtain a leisured and complete view of any person, or object, or place.

It sounds unimportant enough, this vague hindrance which I take to be common to the dreams —I mean, the nocturnal dreams—of all those perpetual dreamers whom we term men and women. Yet it imposed upon me a limitation which debarred the higher reaches of picturesque writing, because upon no occasion during his travels beyond common-sense had the sublime Virginian seen quite enough of anything to provide me with the data for an opulent describing of it.

You may note, as one result of this stumbling-block, that all three of my books about the Peripatetic Episcopalian have been worded, throughout, in somewhat the reserved and homespun style of a scientific thesis, which, in dealing with oneirology, must confine itself to unearthly matters of fact, soberly, without flaunting any trinkets in the shape of "fine writing." Or again, as befits a rational, sound-spirited American who takes in all the better thought-of magazines, you may not know one English prose style from another.

At any rate, although there was no noticed abatement in my friend's customary powers of hearing and of touch, yet three of his five senses were as though drugged—two of them completely, and the other in part—and his reports to me concerning his observations and his various traffics in dreamland were thus maimed.

Moreover—and again, like all of us, I believe

—he retained in his dreaming, in his nocturnal dreaming, no earthly perception of time. For the convenience of the student of this dream trilogy, I during the writing of it suggested here and there a supposed interval of time, just as I philanthropically broke up each book about the Peripatetic Episcopalian into subdivisions, so as to afford breathing spells.

Yet here again, did this all-veracious Virginian remark conclusively,—

"But that is not the way it was."

—For in point of fact, he declared, there were no intervals. Everything appeared to happen almost simultaneously, now that events, and a number of persons too, merged swiftly and unaccountably, but quite naturally, into yet other events and yet other persons; so that the action of his three-faceted dreaming could not really be thought of as coincident with any arithmeticable clock-ticks. It had no alliance with time's passing as we estimate such affairs in earth's daylight.

There seemed, insomuch as my reporting dreamer could phrase the result, to be no particular difference between the length of a year and the length of a vowel and the length of a yardstick. Time had become a matter which (although vaguely perturbing) was unintimate and beyond perception. —For in dreamland you did not travel through time, advancing from one instant to another instant. Instead, so nearly as you could put it, time, hand in hand with chronology, was now travelling about you—moving as if at random rather than exactly backward or forward—at a desultory but broad-minded gait which allowed the potential rights of every known era to be regarded as contemporaneous.

And space also became nomadic. Thus, in your dreaming, you did not ever, not actually, go toward any place, nor did you need to, for the sufficing reason that the place, with an unaccountable complaisance, but still quite naturally, came to you. Just somehow, you were already at that place. You had severed, in brief, all your daylit relations with time and space; and you retained no hidebound or wholly clear conception of either.

It now, to cite but one instance from the first part of this trilogy, appeared unstrange that, in a not quite tangible palace builded out of the finer fabrics of sunset, Charlemagne and Fionn Mac Uail and Prester John and Haroun Al Raschid and Arthur Pendragon should be presiding each at the same instant over the fantastical glories of each monarch's unique entourage, in this gleaming pleasure house which, subject only to your personal choice, graced Aachen, or Tara of the Kings, or Susa, or Baghdad, or Carleon upon Usk.

Nor was this all. That ever, during the aberrations of your waking hours, this circumstance might have seemed out of the ordinary, was a notion which you now recalled with serene wonder, now that this circumstance had to be granted as a matter of unarguable everynight fact which you, with your own personal eyes and ears, were observing in unsurprised approbation.

Throughout the varied course of my friend's dreaming, in short, the simultaneous presence of different places, as well as of different eras, aroused no least sense of incongruity; but had become a phenomenon as self-evident and as unstartling as was the simultaneous presence of all your fingers. —For why, as you reasoned calmly, why, inasmuch as there were always five nimble fingers to each hand, should there not be five noble palaces to each place? Not even to the most obtuse sort of Virginian could the question appear to be otherwise than logical so long as you stayed asleep.

§20. I FORBEAR to cite any further the conditions of a normal dream. To all persons who now and then delight in a sturdy supper these conditions are familiar. I say merely that throughout the trilogy called *The Nightmare Has Triplets* I attempted to conform with the mental and sensory conditions which, to my experience, govern a third of our lives, that superior and immutable third which every human creature needs to pass in dreamland perforce.

I remark likewise that to write truthfully about human dreams is an enterprise which I would recommend to my fellow pedlars of the merchandise we call reading-matter, inasmuch as their mincing avoidance of an entire third of human life appears, to me at any rate, to partake of the squeamish. Moreover do I rejoice to have rectified, at howsoever long a last, my own delinquency in authentic realism.

"In realism," I repeat gravely, and with full consciousness that my remarks here may have misled you into the same quaint error which was committed by the shrill spectres whom Smire met in Acheron. You may well think that hereabouts a bemuddled and out-of-date romance maker is telling you that his own special dream is better than the reality.

And in that case, I can but reply, very much as did the Peripatetic Episcopalian, toward the close of his long journey about the lands beyond common-sense,—

"To the contrary, I am telling you that for humankind the dream is the one true reality."

And I do not know whether or not, by our present-day standards, the dismissive remark of my benignant, all-accomplished, triple-named friend, concerning human dreams, was an intelligent assertion. I know merely that, to my personal finding, it voiced a truth.

All men that live, it is my observance, are condemned to live always in a private, a completely self-evolved dream of one or another nature; and for this fact, I submit, we ought with some emphasis to be grateful. We ought to rejoice whole-heartedly over the circumstance that, as Stevenson has phrased it, "no man lives in the external truth, among salts and acids, but in the warm phantasmagoric chamber of his brain, with the painted windows and the storied walls." The cell of this lifelong prisoner, in brief, can be made quite comfortable, even rococo.

And I know it was upon this all-gladdening fact, or at any rate, upon this article of belief, that my entire dream trilogy was based throughout.

§21. I KNOW FURTHERMORE THAT IF—IF, AS A peevish handful of my reviews reprobated—even if, in some portions of my aforesaid dream trilogy I did touch, just here or there, and in passing, upon conjunctions such as the over-delicate might describe as co-educational exercises, yet was I well justified by their frequency in masculine dreams, and by their imaginary tremendous importance in our first youth and during our prime vigor.

—Though indeed, despite the fact that more staid and elder persons do not talk very much, no, not in public, about the gymnastics which evoked our appearance here upon earth, yet do these quaint antics retain their proper, or if you so prefer it, their improper, status throughout our entire existence, or at any rate through all our terrestrial career, even until gelded and gelding Time, that unamorous jealous censor, has remarked to each of us in turn, one by one,—

REMOTE
EVOLUTION
OF A
ROMANTIC

"Quiet, please."

So they are not negligible. They are likewise, to the best of my recollection, a source of some pleasure. And it follows that if Jehovah, or Who-

soever may, at least possibly, be in charge of this
universe, did indeed invent these gymnastics—
and in fact, recommended them for all living
creatures, so does the church of my faith assure
me, throughout the opening chapter of *The First
Book of Moses, Called Genesis*—why, but in that
case we ought no less freely to praise His fantastic
ingenuity than liberally to avail ourselves thereof,
says logic.

But I have stated previously, now and then, my
grieved opinion as to the now and then unor-
thodox upshot of logic, of all human logic, when
it obtrudes into any human doings, if only just
now and then.

§22. MEANWHILE: in the Virginia of my youth,
the virtue of an unmarried lady—for in those days
this now grotesque word was in standard usage—
hinged wholly upon the integrity of one particular
membrane, so far as went public opinion. In
private, however, as a boy learned by degrees,
nobody believed this; or rather, in private, an
unlegalized loss of virginity among the better
classes, if ever it became discovered, was con-
doned and hushed up by the peccant young
gentlewoman's relatives, by the entire and all-
loyal clan of them, as being, always, due to excep-
tional circumstances for which the broadminded
would make allowance.

Adultery was treated in very much the same way. Everybody acquainted with the involved gentry who had been so injudicious as to become detected would gossip, in private, about the exposure of their illicit amours with an exceeding pleasure. But formally, the existence of any such technical irregularities was not ever recognized, so long as mention of them was "kept out of the newspapers," the local newspapers, one meant. And family influence secured that omission as a matter of course.

I have written elsewhere as to this quaint social rule of thumb, this benevolent hypocrisy. The point here is merely to record gratitude over the fact that my remote youth burgeoned under a prevalence of this so irrational, this so all-accommodating code of morals and of impregnable social standing.

In fairness to myself, or as exactness must phrase it, to this particular one of my former selves, I have need to record also that he did not abuse the prerogatives of this code. When I look back upon the not inconsiderable number of that most serious-minded boy's love-affairs, I in fact believe his physical continence, upon, so to speak, the whole, to have been highly praiseworthy when compared with the run of his contemporaries. They did a lot more of it than you did.

§23. —FOR after you had matured sexually, throughout your latter teens you adhered subconsciously to the code of domnei, or of womanworship, to the belief that the girl with whom, for the instant, you were heels over head in love was sacred and unlike all other girls. With those other girls you did now and then take your rather bungled physical freedoms; but not ever with her during the six months or thereabouts of her regnancy.

You did not want to, somehow; you revered her far too much, as the rule, even to attempt to kiss her. Reflection suggests, nowadays, that some of these ladies in domnei must have found you rather dull company. And never did you, it seems an odd thing nowadays, not ever did you hope to marry her by-and-by. You just simply wanted to be with her as much as was possible, and to write poems about her.

It was a form of worship which you accorded to a dozen, or to be precise about it, to thirteen, girls in succession—but always singly, always sincerely, and with the predecessor of your heart's current occupant dismissed to oblivion. A fair enough use of this callow period was going to be attempted a fair while later on, when a person quite noticeably unlike you began to put together *The Cords of Vanity*. And besides that, still somebody else, an all-domesticated and genteel and a

well contented married man, with stepchildren
almost as old as ever you got to be, revised and
published, a full sixteen years after your extinc-
tion, nearly all the verses which you addressed to
these girls (without ever delivering many of these
verses to their pompadoured and long-petticoated
fair theme) during your college days and your
kerosene lamp lighted night-times, in a book that
he called *From the Hidden Way.*

You were twenty-one, in brief, a romantic-
minded and somewhat moonstruck twenty-one,
before you strayed into the Garden between
Dawn and Sunrise a large number of years before
Jurgen had heard of this place, or you of Jurgen.
There you encountered the original of Dorothy
la Désirée. And that changed all. That was the
primal cause, I suspect nowadays, of your eventually, and through never so many shades of
changing, becoming my collaborator in a rather
huge number of books.

§24. THERE is no saying whether or not the
present-day remnants of that girl whom this yet
other one of my former selves loved utterly
throughout that far-away summer are still wearing
flesh. I could find out, of course. But even though
the last news which I had concerning her, some
five years back, was all-favorable, in that it described her as being "an uncommonly nice and

real sweet old lady," I have no desire to revive
our acquaintance, nor any strong curiosity as to
whether her time-ravaged carcass has been rev-
erently interred or whether it is yet tottering
somewhere upon earth's epidermis. —Because in
any case she would still be three years older than
I, and (I am certain) she would still smell more
or less faintly of perspiration under her armpits.
She always did.

I am grateful to her for that wholly happy
summer and autumn throughout which a delectable blonde wanton incited and shared a more
passionate delight than ever anyone of the several
different persons who since then have inhabited
my body was destined to find anywhere. I am
grateful, now, for the longheadedness, the bland
intelligence, with which toward the end of the
ensuing November—for her letter, sent by special
delivery, arrived with an ironic patness upon
Thanksgiving Day—she dismissed that twenty-
one years' old penniless youngster in order to
marry a partially lame, age-stricken person (who,
in fact, was well on in his thirties) with a sub-
stantial bank account. And I am far more than
grateful for the enraged misery which the bewildered young man then faced.

—Because, I reflect, these prehistoric matters
altered all his excessive notions about women,
with highly pleasurable results, by and large. This

changing I take to have been the direct origin of the book called *Jurgen*; and throughout a dozen years this changing afforded a fine deal of material which eventually got into yet other books.

Now, this changing I find to be remarked on, and accurately enough, in the fourth chapter of *Jurgen*, where the aging pawnbroker is ascribing to his own past this identical changing.

"Oh, but it was armor that hour brought him, and a humor to use it, because no woman now could hurt him very seriously. No, never any more! . . . And women, as he knew by experience now, were the pleasantest of playfellows. So he began to play . . . and with many brightly colored playmates who took the game more seriously than he did."

Yes; all this happened to my aforetime self more than a half-century ago and during the twelve years which followed, those not unhappy years throughout which he shared his pleasure-seeking, and his pleasure-giving also, I elect to hope, with various gentlewomen, sedately and fearlessly, because he was certain that never again would he become inconveniently fond of a woman. He was wrong there; but not for twelve twelvemonths did he discover this circumstance.

Meanwhile, he very much enjoyed his discreet love-affairs, these tonic love-dealings which strengthened his writing. And he really owed

every one of them, in addition to the book called
Jurgen, along with yet many other books, so do I
reflect nowadays, to the intelligent, ivory-colored,
high-nosed and yellow-haired, perspiratory young
gentlewoman who had flouted him in his twenty-
second year.

It follows that I am quite properly grateful to
her—nowadays—for having, as the cliché puts it,
broken his heart. —Especially because it did not
stay broken.

§25. TO THE contrary. His main interest, in fact
(excluding always his need to be writing, which
ranked always above all else), had shifted from
his heart to less publicized organs. And his
Dorothy la Désirée, he began to think, was pretty
much like other girls.

Of course, though (as he by-and-by was reminding himself, in the sober twilight of unsuc-
cess), there were right many of them with whom
you couldn't get anywhere. Some girls would not
even let you kiss them. But they did not really
mind your having tried to kiss them, or your
having attempted yet closer intimacies. They
would make you stop, and they would tell you
how they most certainly hoped that nothing which
they had ever said or done could have led you,
not even for one single solitary moment, to think
about such a thing. But just the same, they took it

as a sort of compliment, you noticed; and you got along all right with them, afterwards, just being friends.

To the other side, my ci-devant self had found out—experimentally, and for a rather longish while with, as I remember it, a now pathetic seeming surprise—that a fair number of accessible young gentlewomen whose social standing stayed unquestioned, whether as wives or as spinsters, were no whit averse to extreme amorous dalliance if only you took sane precautions as to there not being, by-and-by, any embarrassing sequel in infant form. And so when they once let you begin hugging and kissing them, then you did not have to let that be all.

No, not if only you kept on talking and talking in the right way about how very much you were in love with her, and did not pay any attention when she said, "But we mustn't, dear," and told you please, please to stop. —Because she did not mean one word of it, not really. So you could just keep right on.

That is a bit too naively phrased, perhaps. But in practice among the upper circles of the state of Virginia the young man about whom I am thinking, that apostate from domnei, found it to be fair enough psychology; and in theory—or as an hypothesis, anyhow—I too believe that these principles, or as it may be one ought to call them, these unprinciples, stay sound.

I incline, in short, to agree with Balzac (although merely as a general rule which, like every other general rule, has its due number of exceptions) that the virtue of women is man's most pleasing invention. —Which is but to say that no healthy normal young woman anywhere has an innate trend toward chastity, it is my belief.

Yet I speak with a proper diffidence. I speak modestly and humbly, after confessing that in person I have not tested these unprinciples for a multitude of years. So I do not know anything, not assuredly, not with an intimateness, about the young women of today; and it well may be that my gallant faith in them, like my even more early chivalrous delusions as to all gentlewomen, now sounds old-fashioned.

§26. AT ANY RATE, I CANNOT BUT LOOK BACK UPON the hurtless and the so ancient love-traffics of that beginning author with a complacent wonder as to his and my thrift. —For of almost every young woman who figured in them (so do I address his ghost) your memories were utilized in one or another book.

They are long ago forgotten books, there is no denying, so far as concerns the devotees of Francis X. Flubberdub and of Gideon Gibberish and of Natalie Babu English and of Laura Caconym Nugatory. Still, we enjoyed writing our books, we enjoyed it savoringly. That is the main point, the point for which today I am grateful.

IN PRAISE OF AN EXCEEDING ECONOMY

You alone were the author, so do I estimate, of the first nine volumes to appear under our shared name. I cannot feel I had any particular hand in them, beyond more or less fondly and painstakingly revising their texts so many years later. My own first book, so do I believe, was *The Cream of the Jest*.

Nevertheless, long after I had become an all-domesticated and genteel and a well contented husband who (as I have recorded in another

place) in almost every one of his writings por-
trayed something of his own wife in that feminine
character to whom his protagonist was married,
still even then did I retain your memories of
various other, once very dear young women; and
of these memories I in my turn made use, just as
you had made use of them, in the most thrifty and
business-like fashion conceivable, a fashion such
as today I find it edifying to consider. —For of
late I have been adventuring through the obsolete
and oblivion-devoured volumes written by each
one of us, so as to appraise in particular the female
characters therein. And none of them appears to
be a complete invention; each more or less has
been colored by recollection.

At times, so far as I can now distinguish, everything, alike in the fictional young woman's physical appearance and her nature, seems to have
been copied all from one person—as with Mar-
garet Hugonin in *The Eagle's Shadow*, or with
Dorothy la Désirée, as well as Guenevere, in
Jurgen, or with both Bettie Hamlyn and Gillian
Hardress in *The Cords of Vanity*. Or again, this
or the other young woman would afford a brief
description of her person, or a remembered bit of
her speaking, or for that matter, a sentence or so
from some letter which she had written to you.

One letter alone did you preserve in full, the
final letter from her whom we with discretion

may continue to term your Dorothy la Désirée. It in the way of unhappiness had meant a great deal to you at the time of its receipt. And so in *The Cords of Vanity* you attributed this epoch-inaugurating letter to Avis M. Beechinor, changing not any syllable of it, except only the proper names, but exaggerating somewhat her tendency toward misspellings. And you appended to it, from the mouth of plump Robert Etheridge Townsend, a suitable commentary.

Sometimes there were odd alterings, as when Mr. Townsend's Elena Barry-Smith is presented as a blonde, although in reality the once upon a time, through two whole summers, adored young divorcée (adored, though, with intermissions) who posed for her looked very much like Claire de Puysange, in that painstaking description of the latter which, in the final version of *Gallantry*, needed to be abridged, and with a howsoever well-nigh regretful rigorousness, because of Mr. John Bulmer's a page- and one-half-ful consideration of her features, and of their effects upon him, both spiritual and cardiac, having delayed most awkwardly Mr. John Bulmer's proposal of marriage.

Upon yet other occasions, two of those so long extinct young darlings—for in sober truth each of them, it now seems to me, was really a darling, temporarily—have been blended into one person. And lastly, the self-same gentlewoman, or at any rate some fragments of her, can be found surviving under a new alias from one book into another book, as when Marian Heleigh quits the pages of *Gallantry,* to enter *The Cords of Vanity* as Gillian Hardress, and a while later intrudes into *The Cream of the Jest* as Muriel Allardyce; or as when, most notably, that Claire Bulmer Townsend, who figures briefly in *The Cords of Vanity* as Mr. Townsend's flibberty-gibbet young mother, after contributing to Patricia Stapylton throughout *The Rivet in Grandfather's Neck,* becomes Melior in *The High Place,* then gets into *The First Gentleman of America* (more or less) as Doña Antonia, and rounds off all in *There Were Two Pirates,* by turning into Isabel de Castro. Economy could not very well go farther.

So your not always licit love-affairs (I concede to this so long dead young fellow) proved in the end to be sound enough investments of your spare moments and of your caressing—and even of each of your almost quite serious, babbled and high-flown protestations—in that, forever afterward, this seeming gallimaufry of nonsense paid us unfailing dividends, in the form of never so intimate memories of divers generous-natured and alluringly tinted young feminine persons, such as both of us could write about henceforward with a tolerable amount of assurance.

Both of us, I repeat. —Because even I, who am so unlike you nowadays, I who seem to have stumbled somehow into becoming a wholly virtuous and all-sedate incarnate infirmity, with this or the other deteriorative slight ailment beyond arithmetic, I can still remember, and rather vividly at that, what each of those so injudicious young women who wasted their time on you was like, in body and in speech and in kindliness.

§27. YET UPON SECOND THOUGHT I AM NOT SURE their time was wasted. —For you addressed to them, convincingly, a vast deal of high-pitched and highly flattering nonsense which you also believed, at least partly, to be true enough; and they liked hearing it. Your caresses were competent. And before long they had been adorned with a satisfying technique.

Well, and the result was that your comely panting opponents, one after another, appeared each and all of them, to the very best of my recollection, to enjoy quite wholeheartedly the exchange of a number of varied intimacies.

So it may be that, even though nothing whatever, nothing tangible except only some fifty books and book-

CONCERNING
MANY
LONG DEAD
PERSONS

lets, came of your love-affairs, yet the young women who figured in them did not really squander the time during which, like you and me, they may have acquired a thesaurus of pleasure-giving and heart-warming and yet, yet, of somehow half-wistful memories.

—Or at least I hope so. It is pleasing to consider you a benefactor; and to both you and me these so long evanished young women have been beneficent in this special fashion, now for more than a half century. And besides that—here once again to become practical—they bequeathed to each of us all these dear memories as a most useful theme for our writing.

In theory, inasmuch as a number of your love-affairs involved adultery or, in some instances, a technical seduction, they were unpraiseworthy. Yet, as I cannot but reflect, and must concede to you in bare justice, nothing whatever came of them except a most lively allowance of pleasure —and book after book.

No harm came of them, no scandal of any nature, or at least no widely gossiped-about scandal such as had to be "kept out of the news-papers." The husbands of the wedded gentle-women concerned were each spared forever after-ward, I am certain, any knowledge which might have proved distasteful. And of the four former virgins, three acquired husbands by-and-by, with whom to live in contentment, so far as went every appearance, for the remainder of their shared existence.

One of them, indeed, became the wife of a personage so tolerably well known that now and then I was privileged to see him later on in the news reels. I, being both human and auctorial, I resented, I suppose, my supplanter's famousness.

Yet always did these haphazard, brief, stray glimpses of him, so very many years after her death, awake in me a certain sense of nostalgia —along with an uncertain sense of complacency, along with an uncertain wonder as to just how much, during his first honeymoon, the big-jowled, lumbering, so blank-eyed man ever did, or else didn't, discover.

She was a most tactful girl, always; and I suspect that as a bride she remained tactful.

Nor, nowadays, can any particular damage rise from my being thus frank as to your love-affairs —except only, of course, my being accredited, among the obtuse, with an obtuse, boastful and repugnant, lewd egotism. It is a rebuking to which I am not un-casehardened. In truth, though, I myself, the current I, did not have anything at all to do with these amorous goings-on; and the detachment with which I regard them is glacial.

—For I deal with ancient history, I speak as to the doings of a beginning author of whom no particle survives anywhere today, whereas the soft-lipped girls with whom he junketed are in reality as dead as Cleopatra or as Eve or as Catherine the Great. Not every one of them has gone through the formality of a funeral, with flowers and the proper cards of condolence, to be sure; but nothing endures of their comeliness, or of their dearness, in the gray gentlewomen, the austere grandmothers usually, whom they have become under time's handling. I dislike these old ladies, mildly; but we get along together well enough, "just being friends."

My point, however, and my salutary true moral, is that although in general your conduct (you so long-ago deceased youngster) all seems, nowadays, to have been unimportant and so foolish, and so childish even, I know that—merely as a regrettable axiom, merely as is the granted inability of twice two ever to vary very much from fourness—I know most assuredly, that it wasn't. I know that your evolution was, in all its essentials, the evolution of each and of every other predestined male writer, those persons for whom writing is inevitable. So far as go the female practitioners of authorship, I prefer to cough and pass on without committing myself.

Hence, then, am I being candid about you. You did that which every "born" male writer, whether living or dead, has done always out of naked necessity. And therefore, therefore alone, do I regard your story as being of some noteworthy importance, not, heaven knows, because it happened to you, but because it happens, such is my belief, in every one of those psychopathic cases which by-and-by result in professional authorship. (To authoresses I do not allude, I needs here repeat cautiously.) I regard you, sir, in fine, as being alike a parable and a case history —and indeed, as being a compendium of all those male writers who at all matter, such as, for an instance, even Francis X. Flubberdub and Gideon Gibberish.

Now I do not mean merely that the two of us have utilized your memories as to those extinct young women, these present-day grandmothers, again and yet again in our fictions. —For a writer, as I have said earlier, must utilize nearly every one of his acquaintances, in the end, under this or the other disguise, howsoever flimsy; and he does so without scruple. It is a condition of our trade.

I mean, rather, that the "born" writer requires a number of women, just as you did, during the prime of his physical vigor. And he requires them, primarily—such is my point—because his love-affairs will render how very far more keen his sensitiveness, not only throughout a horde of bed-room sports, but toward all his surroundings, toward all nature, toward most emotions. Instinctively he thus turns to women, because they stimulate and they sustain his power to write, which, after all, is what he in chief wants to do, or perhaps even, for some inscrutable reason, that goal to attain which he was created.

Here is no question of morality, and no plea for a writer's particular license in such affairs, but the mere statement of what I take to be a fact. The male writer whose alliance with his art is cordial will make use of many women unknowingly— and very often with an at any rate almost complete faith in his devotion to them, one by one, in a sort of serialized harem—because his contacts with women and because a sufficiency, or rather, let us so name it, a glut, of love-dealings, no matter whether they should turn out to be joyful or disastrous, will increase his power to write. The "born" writer divines this much by intuition, so do I believe, without ever needing to word it to anybody, or, in especial, to himself.

And I am sure likewise that I do not know how he divines it, nor why it should be a most certain, a wholly undesirable, truth. But I do know that it is.

§28. HOWEVER! you, my ci-devant and restless, wilding self, you expired, painlessly and with large contentment, at the Rockbridge Alum Springs, amidst the demure Alleghany mountains of Virginia, during the August of 1912, when I met the brown-haired young woman who, before long, became my first wife. But of that encounter in an ancient sunset I have written elsewhere, in yet another tiny volume, not ever published, as well as of the unspeakable dear commonplace blessings which it procured for me throughout the thirty-five years and four months of my married life with her.

—Or rather, now that one comes to think of the affair more justly, it was you who married her. I, who existed thenceforward, under her loving dominance, as an all-domesticated and genteel and a wholly contented person, I was, but how entirely, a by-product of your marriage! And in consequence (says logic, our old friend), I must rank as your posthumous offspring.

—So that I should endeavor, it follows still in strict logic, to approach your memory with a rather more filial sort of hypocrisy than I have shown thus far, and with much more reverence than at heart I can ever feel for you, or for logic either.

§29. YET IS IT REQUIRED OF ALL US UNDER-graduates of the mortician's parlor, so do I reflect, not to flout common-sense, not permanently. It follows that for the life of me, and on my conscience, I fail to regret your part in any one of those ancient, ardent, not wholly un-hole-and-cornerish, but remunerative and, as I think, inevitable love-matters; nor may I consider them to have displayed any special sinister tints of double-dyed iniquity.

You and this or the other reasonably goodlooking, reasonably intelligent young woman were drawn to each other in your shared youth; and the two of you then gratified your desire for each other, getting out of youth as much pleasure as was possible, before youth had

WHICH, AT LAST, BECOMES RATIONAL

quitted the two of you forever. Technically, no matter whether your vis-à-vis was married or not, it was wrong, by the nominal standards of your day, as well as by today's more liberal standards; but in the outcome, says logic, it proved to be wisdom also. The lives of both of you were enriched; our books, our so very many books, were made viable; and nobody else was any least whit the worse for it.

Should anyone of our fellow Episcopalians confront us with the Seventh Commandment, so does logic continue—and to the fidgeting disapproval of my present-day correctness in the genteel—then we can but cite the Sixth. "Thou shalt not kill" is no less explicit, no shade less uncompromising, than "Thou shalt not commit adultery." The same Sinaic authority endorses each of these rules of personal etiquette. Yet we all grant (except only a few despised slackers) that to kill may become the most high and holy duty of a sound citizen. To this sacrosanct sole end are his armaments mustered, his atomic bombs devised, his belt tightened, his sons immolated, and his taxes multiplied, all with his rector's full approval.

In fact—for here again breaks in that so pertinacious logic—reflection can detect no one of the ten commandments which is regarded with an unflawed and absolute, or at least an unconditional, seriousness, nowadays. They do not jibe, not always, with modern conceptions, we feel tacitly. —For when once you come to think about it (logic continues), the Decalogue does begin by denying freedom of religion; it voices a quaint deal of uncivilized taboos, such as about not working on Saturday or, upon any terms, condoning the arts of sculpture or painting; and it terminates with an order which, apart from the

impossibility of anyone's obedience thereto so
long as men and women retain human nature,
would end all business enterprise, and demolish
alike every known trade and profession. There is
no form of common-sense endeavor but is begotten, and is spurred on toward completion, by
coveting one's neighbor's money or something
yet other of that which is his, remarks logic
conclusively.

§30. A FAINT regret, though, I do feel that, after
your infatuation for the original of Dorothy la
Désirée was over and well done with, you so soon
heart-whole youngster, you never, to the best of
my recollection, "fell in love" with anybody. You
were not ever fulfilled with any such phrenetic
passion as all the poets and most of the novelists
of yesterday tell about; and with time you began
to doubt if any such passion indeed exists.

Certainly, you were never troubled by it. You
were fond of one young woman after another.
Your affection in each case was sincere. You
admired your heart's, or at any rate your incli-
nation's, current sovereign for one or another
perfectly sound reason; and you delighted to
make love to her, both physical and declamatory.

Yet always your protestations were, as you well
knew, a tinge over-colored. It was a sort of game,
a sort of play-acting, a ritual of courtship, and a

most enjoyable affair throughout. But it was not at all like that reputed "falling in love."

I imagine, nowadays, that such is every young male's, and it may be, every young woman's experience. I imagine that, in mere point of fact, and no matter how varied may be his transactions in amour, nobody ever does really "fall in love" with the ardor and the amplitude which so very many of our best-thought-of writers describe with glibness.

Yet I do not know about this, of course. Nor, I daresay, does anyone else. —For it is our fate here on earth, I repeat, to know but one person with any least true intimacy. A man does know, that is, something about himself; and as befits a sensible creature, he at once begins to prevaricate about himself, especially in his reveries.

He learns also how to lie flatly to himself, and with time to convince himself, concerning his intimacy with this or with that or with the other person, rather than to face his complete loneliness inside that cell which we term a skull. That those of his fellow beings who are most close and dearest to him must none the less remain always a mixture of radio announcements fetched in by his unreliable five senses, the prisoner (again, as befits a sensible creature) refuses to acknowledge.

No man anywhere may dare to face the thought

of that actual loneliness; it is a truism which sanity compels us to disregard; and for that reason I now dismiss this unpleasant truism. I decline to believe any word of it.

—Because nowadays, in common with my betters, I too avoid always a full-face confronting of undesired realities. I prefer instead to regard, and to give reverent thanks for, the large host of rather pleasant happenings in which, to my own experience at any rate, our human living here upon earth is fertile.

And youth is the chief of them. Youth happens to everybody. Youth is a wholly commonplace phenomenon. Young persons (as indeed perhaps you may have noted) are to be encountered almost everywhere. Nevertheless is youth a miracle, a most enjoyable miracle, a benevolent tour de force, so do I elect to believe, upon heaven's part.

Hence does it follow, nowadays, that I stay all-grateful to Jehovah, or to Whosoever may, at least possibly, be in charge of this universe, because I too was young in it, a long while ago, throughout a fond glad while before Time had remarked, in regard to my youth, and to its varied activities, and to all its never so pleasant nonsense,—

"Quiet, please."

EXPLICIT